All of a sudden Betsy grew serious. "Okay, Sam. I think that now it's time for me and Carla to tell you about the *other* side of baby-sitting."

"The other side?" This didn't sound good.

"I think what Betsy means," Carla said slowly, "is that all kids are not exactly angels."

"That's an understatement." Betsy cried. "I once had a little girl pour a whole bottle of glue on my head!"

"I once had a little boy sneak into the kitchen while I was busy playing Uncle Wiggly with his two sisters upstairs in their bedroom. He ate an entire half gallon of chocolate ice cream." Carla rolled her eyes. "He was sick for three days. And boy, was his mother mad at me!"

"That's nothing," Betsy said. "What about the time a set of twins I was sitting for decided to surprise their parents by painting pictures all over the hallway? Talk about an angry mother!"

"Paint? Ice Cream? Glue?" I gulped. "Why didn't you two tell me about any of this before?"

"Oh, it's not always like that," Betsy assured me.

WARNING: BABY-SITTING MAY BE HAZARDOUS TO YOUR HEALTH

Cynthia Blair

FAWCETT JUNIPER • NEW YORK

RLI: $\dfrac{\text{VL 4 \& up}}{\text{IL 5 \& up}}$

A Fawcett Juniper Book
Published by Ballantine Books
Copyright © 1993 by Cynthia Blair

Library of Congress Catalog Card Number: 92-97068

ISBN 0-449-70412-2

Manufactured in the United States of America

First Edition: March 1993

chapter
one

"Flowers, candles, crystal . . . Who's coming to dinner tonight, the president of the United States?"

My older sister, Elizabeth, managed to say exactly what *I* had been thinking. We had just come home from school, each of us lugging an armful of books. We'd been planning to pass right through the dining room and head into the kitchen for a snack. But the elegant way the table was set stopped us in our tracks.

"Forget the president," I said. "How about the queen of England?"

Our housekeeper, Bonnie, had set the table with all our best. The tablecloth was an heirloom, cream-colored lace tatted by hand in Belgium. The china and crystal were the family's finest. Bonnie had even brought out the antique silverware, the set that had been in the Langtree family for six generations. She must have spent the entire morning polishing it, because it was as shiny as a mirror.

In the middle of the table was a huge bouquet of cream-colored roses, almost the exact same shade as the tablecloth. On both sides of the huge crystal vase were silver candlesticks with pink candles in them, as long and graceful as the roses.

All this for a regular old Wednesday evening in early October.

My mother came hurrying into the dining room. "Does everything look all right?" she asked nervously. She surveyed the room, then leaned across the table and tore one brown-edged leaf off the otherwise perfect roses.

Our dining room table wasn't the only thing that was all decked out. Mother was wearing a blue silk dress, one she saved for special occasions. And as I was quickly coming to realize, something along the lines of a "special occasion" was definitely in the works here in the Langtree household.

"I want everything to be perfect for tonight," Mother said. "Your father invited one of his old school friends for dinner. Ellsworth von Thornbottom is coming over with his wife, Bootsy, and their two daughters, Bethany and Clarissa. As a matter of fact, Samantha, I believe that Clarissa is about your age. She's twelve or thirteen. And Bethany is your age, Elizabeth. She's fifteen, just like you."

Bethany von Thornbottom? Clarissa von Thornbottom? My heart sank. Believe me, with a name like Samantha Langtree—a name that I have been told sounds like something out of a book . . . a book about a spoiled rich girl, that is—I know that I'm hardly in a position to go around drawing conclusions about people based on their names. But mine suddenly seemed as ordinary as Mary Jones compared to Bethany and Clarissa von Thornbottom.

"Excuse me, girls," said Mother. "I'd better go check on Bonnie. She's making Rock Cornish hen with truffles, and I want to make sure she doesn't go overboard with the herbs."

My sister and I just looked at each other. Rock Cornish hen? Truffles? This *was* a special occasion.

"By the way," Mother called over her shoulder, "I expect you both to wear your very best outfits this evening. And when Katherine comes in, please tell her to do the same. After all, she's in the fifth grade now, certainly old enough to start dressing up for dinner."

All of a sudden, I had this overwhelming urge to call up Betsy Crane, one of my two best friends in the world. That was because I was finding myself in need of some major moral support. Whenever that happens, I call upon the other members of the Bubble Gum Gang.

I guess I'd better go back. The Bubble Gum Gang is the name of this little group I belong to. "Little" is probably an understatement, since there are only three of us who belong. There's me, of course. And Betsy Crane, who's as smart as a whip, as the old saying goes. She's always been the top student in her class, sometimes even being labeled "teacher's pet."

The third member is Carla Farrell. Dear, sweet Carla Farrell, who wants more than anything to be a great actress when she grows up. There's one minor thing standing in her way—and that's the fact that Carla is a few pounds overweight. But she's working on it. And with me and Betsy behind her, cheering her on, none of us has a bit of doubt that she's going to reach her goal.

You see, helping one another out is a big part of what the Bubble Gum Gang is all about. In fact, one of the main reasons we banded together in the first place was that all three of us had a long history of being social outcasts. Betsy because she's always been so brainy, Carla because of her weight . . . and me because I happen to be the middle daughter in the Langtree family, the wealthiest family in Hanover.

I'm not saying that to brag. True, belonging to the family that lives in the biggest house in town, owns the fanciest car, and goes on exotic vacations to places like London and Rome and the south of France has certainly had its advantages. But in one way all that has been a big *disadvantage*. In terms of fitting in with the other kids my age, being the richest girl in town has always set me apart from everybody else.

And that's the last thing I've ever wanted. In fact, I've gone out of my way to be friendly. But somehow the other girls at Hanover Elementary School always saw me as a show-off. A snob. Somebody who thought she was better than everybody else. Since I could never manage to convince them they were wrong, I ended up spending a lot of time alone, reading, horseback riding, and simply daydreaming.

And then, suddenly, all that changed. I started the seventh grade at Hanover Junior High. During the first couple of weeks of school, Betsy and Carla and I just kind of found one another. The rest, as they say, is history. A brand-new friendship sprang up. The Bubble Gum Gang was born.

Being friends is only part of it. The three of us also share an interest in solving mysteries and going off on adventures and helping out whoever needs helping out. Whenever we can, that is. We always have our eyes open, hoping for an adventure or a mystery to come our way. But a lot of the time, we three members of the Bubble Gum Gang just hang out together, having a lot of fun. We're pals, and that means supporting one another, no matter what problems any of us are facing.

Which is one of the main reasons I thought of calling Betsy the moment I began to dread the elegant dinner with the von Thornbottoms.

"Hi, Betsy," I said brightly as soon as she picked up the telephone. "What's new?"

"What's new?" Betsy laughed. "Samantha, it's only been—let me see—seventeen minutes since I saw you coming out of the school building. All that's happened since then is that I walked home, came into our lovely apartment here at Clifton Garden Homes, and began making myself a peanut butter and jelly sandwich. Now, isn't that the most exciting thing you've ever heard in your life?"

I let out a long sigh. "I guess I just wanted to hear a familiar voice," I told her. "A *friendly*, familiar voice."

Betsy immediately picked up on my mood. "What's wrong, Samantha? I'm getting the feeling that while my last seventeen minutes were not very interesting, your last seventeen minutes *were*."

"Oh, it's no big deal, really. It's just that when my sister and I walked into the house, we found that Bonnie and my mother were acting as if royalty were coming to dinner. Flowers, candles, our best silverware . . . the whole bit.''

''What's wrong with that?'' Betsy asked. ''If you ask me, a fancy dinner party sounds like fun.''

''It's the guest list that bothers me. My father invited an old school friend of his to dinner, along with his whole family. I've heard him mention this man, Ellsworth von Thornbottom, before—''

''Ellsworth von Thornbottom?'' Betsy repeated.

I could tell from her voice that she wasn't sure if she'd heard me correctly.

''You've got it. And apparently this guy is exactly the way his name sounds. Filthy rich, and he wants everybody to know it. He made a fortune in business, manufacturing hair ornaments, of all things. But that's not even the worst of it.'' I took a deep breath. ''He's bringing his two teenage daughters, Clarissa and Bethany. And Elizabeth and Katherine and I are expected to play hostess to them.''

''Well . . . maybe they'll be nice,'' Betsy said hopefully. ''I mean, just because their father is full of himself, that doesn't mean his daughters won't turn out to be okay.''

''I suppose you're right.'' I sighed. ''I should at least give them a chance.''

''That's the spirit!'' Betsy said heartily. ''And who knows? Maybe you'll like Clarissa and Bethany so much that you'll be calling me back in a few hours, telling me you want to invite them to join the Bubble Gum Gang.''

Betsy and I both laughed. But that didn't mean I

got rid of the feeling of dread that was sitting smack in the middle of my stomach. As a matter of fact, as I hung up the phone, I found myself wishing I were at Betsy's, snacking on peanut butter and jelly sandwiches instead of getting ready for a dinner of Rock Cornish hen and truffles with two girls named Bethany and Clarissa von Thornbottom.

"Ellsworth. Bootsy. Come on in!"

My father was playing the role of the perfect host as he opened the front door and invited his guests in. I, meanwhile, was standing on the stairs in the front entryway. So were my older sister Elizabeth and my younger sister Katherine. All three of us were peering over the top of the banister, eager to get a look at our guests.

Betsy's words were still echoing through my head. "Maybe they'll be nice," she had said. "Just because their father is full of himself, that doesn't mean his daughters won't turn out to be okay."

I only hoped she was right.

"Great to see you, Bill." Ellsworth von Thornbottom had just come in, his larger-than-life presence filling the room. He was a tall, heavyset man with a big stomach bulging over the top of his belt. He talked just a little bit too loudly, and he was smoking a cigar. In his hands was a large cardboard box.

His wife, Bootsy, meanwhile, was the exact opposite. She filed in after him, smiling but not saying a word. She was small and blond, dressed in a simple expensive-looking dress that was practically hidden by all the gold jewelry she was wearing. She, too, was carrying a box, although hers was white. It was printed in pink with the name of a French bakery.

But it was their daughters I was most interested in. I craned my neck forward, trying to get a look.

The feeling of dread that had been sitting in my stomach suddenly blew up like a balloon.

"My, my, what a charming *little* home!" gushed one of the girls—probably Clarissa, I figured, since she looked about my age. "Is this your summer-house?"

My mother answered her graciously. "Why, no, dear. This is . . . this is where we live." She was wearing a big smile, but I could tell she had been caught off guard.

"I just *adore* these smaller places," said the other girl, Bethany. "They're so . . . so *quaint*."

Both Bethany and Clarissa were dressed to the hilt. They looked as if they were going to a ball, practically, instead of just going over to somebody's house for dinner on a Wednesday night. They were wearing fancy dresses—Bethany's was velvet, and Clarissa's looked like silk—along with stockings and high heels. They had on gobs of makeup, and their hair had so much mousse in it I figured they must have set their alarm clocks for six o'clock that morning just to start putting it in.

"Samantha, Katherine, Elizabeth, come down and meet our guests," my mother called. The cheerful-ness in her voice sounded forced. Dutifully the three of us came down—out of our safety zone. I swallowed hard. I could already tell that we were all in for a long night.

"These are my daughters," my mother was saying. "Samantha, Katherine, Elizabeth . . ."

Clarissa's face fell. "Oh, dear," she said. "Are we too early? I can see you haven't had time to dress."

It was all I could do to keep my mouth from dropping open. You see, I was wearing the very best dress I own, a simple blue one with a few ruffles here and there. I had gotten it in England the winter before. That dress always makes me feel like Alice in Wonderland, especially since I have long blond hair almost to my waist and blue eyes almost the same color as the fabric. I was also wearing my favorite shoes, pink ones that look like ballet slippers.

I decided to ignore Clarissa's obnoxious comment. "It's nice to meet you," I said, trying my best to sound friendly.

Clarissa just sniffed the air.

"We'd better get this into the refrigerator." Bootsy von Thornbottom, the girls' mother, had finally spoken. "I simply couldn't resist bringing dessert. I always find it such *fun* to help out. But don't keep it out. Fresh cream simply does not keep." She let out a little giggle.

"Here, I brought something, too." Ellsworth von Thornbottom handed the box he had been carrying to my father. "Hair ornaments, for your daughters. The Thornbottom Corporation just acquired three or four new companies, and this is a sampling of the product line of one of them."

"How thoughtful of you, Ellsworth," said my mother. "Now, why don't you girls go into the den while we grown-ups get comfortable in the living room?'' She gave me a desperate look. ''That way, you can all have fun getting to know one another.''

''You have a *den*?'' Clarissa said.

''Sure,'' I replied. ''It's where we keep the TV and the VCR.''

Clarissa tossed her head. ''*We* call that the media center.''

Just then, my older sister leaned over in my direction and whispered, ''Sam, would you mind terribly if I pretended I had suddenly gotten an awful headache?''

''You'd better not leave me alone with these two,'' I whispered back. ''If you do, I'll never talk to you again.''

Elizabeth glanced over at Bethany, who was running her finger along a table, as if checking for dust. She held up the finger, glanced at it, and made a face. ''You know, Sam, I think it might almost be worth it.''

''So,'' I began brightly, once we were all sitting together in the den—a room I would never in a million years be able to bring myself to call a ''media center.'' ''Where do you go to school?''

''*L'école des jeunes filles de Genève*,'' Bethany replied in a matter-of-fact voice.

''What?'' squealed my little sister, Katherine. ''Say it in English!''

Clarissa cast her a dirty look. ''It's French for the Geneva School for Girls.'' She gave one of her little sniffs, then added, ''It's in Switzerland.''

"What about you?" From the way Bethany said the words, I could tell she really couldn't care less.

"We all go to the public school right here in town," I said.

"*Public* school!" both Clarissa and Bethany cried in unison.

"Whatever for?" Clarissa asked.

"We like our school," Elizabeth said, her voice a little more high-pitched than usual. "It's a wonderful place!"

I gave her arm a little squeeze. I was trying to tell her, Elizabeth, don't even waste your breath.

The rest of the evening proceeded in pretty much the same way. From what I could see over dinner, my mother was having just as hard a time being nice to the snobby Bootsy von Thornbottom as my sisters and I were having acting friendly toward Bethany and Clarissa. Only my father seemed to be having a good time, talking about "the good old days" with his childhood friend, Ellsworth.

Aside from dragging up stories from the Middle Ages, when the two of them were kids, Mr. von Thornbottom's favorite subject seemed to be how much money he had. He was very clever about letting everybody know about it, sneaking it into the conversation so that he didn't really sound as if he were bragging. He complained about how hard it was to find a good garage mechanic to repair Italian sports cars. He insisted that we all simply *had* to try skiing in the mountains of Africa. He spent a good five minutes trying to figure out exactly how many times he had traveled around the world.

I felt as if the evening were never going to end.

"Everyone ready for dessert?" Mother finally asked. Bonnie had just cleared the table, and my mother came in from the kitchen, carrying a big plate. On it was what looked like a strawberry shortcake. Only it was the biggest, fanciest-looking strawberry shortcake I had ever seen in my life.

"Everyone simply *must* have some of that *marvelous* strawberry velvet supreme," gushed Bethany.

"Oh, yes!" Clarissa cooed. "It's simply too, too divine!"

"It was shipped from the most exclusive bakery in Paris," Bethany added. "Royalty shops there."

I glanced over at their mother, who was smiling at her little dears approvingly. "I can hardly wait to try it," I said, but neither Bethany nor Clarissa seemed to have heard me.

My mother had set it down on the table. "I'll make sure to cut each of you a generous slice," she said, smiling at the von Thornbottom girls.

"Oh, no! None for me!" Dramatically, Bethany held up her hands.

I just looked at her.

My mother also looked confused. "Excuse me, Bethany?"

"I said, none for me."

"Me, either," Clarissa insisted. She was also waving her hands in front of her, as if trying to chase away something evil. "I hardly *ever* eat sweets."

Bethany wrinkled her nose. "I don't want to gain weight. If I did, I wouldn't fit into all the gorgeous designer clothes my sweet, wonderful daddy is always buying me.''

"*Especially* since we're planning another shopping trip to Paris this winter,'' Clarissa added with a giggle. "And *you* know how those European clothes are made. Why, one piece of strawberry velvet supreme and the lines of this year's designs would be totally *ruined*.''

By that point, my mouth had dropped open so far that my lower lip was practically dragging on Mother's handmade lace tablecloth.

"Hey, Elizabeth?'' I whispered, leaning over toward my sister.

"Yes, Sam?''

"You know that imaginary headache of yours?''

"Yes?''

I let out a sigh. "I think it's contagious.''

Even though I had begun to worry that the von Thornbottoms were never going to leave, eventually they did. I let out a loud sigh of relief, then walked around the house, switching off lights.

"I guess it was fun for you, seeing your old school chum,'' I commented to my father. My mother and my sisters had already gone upstairs to get ready for bed, leaving me and my father alone to lock up the house. I, meanwhile, was trying to be a good sport about the long, terrible evening we had all just endured.

Instead of the hearty, "Oh, yes,'' I had been expecting, he let out a loud sigh of his own.

"Well, I guess you could say the evening was an education," he finally replied.

"An education?" I repeated. "What do you mean?"

"Seeing Ellsworth again, after so many years—and especially meeting his daughters—showed me how having a lot of money can turn out to be a bad thing."

I had to agree. "It certainly seems to be all that Clarissa and Bethany care about, doesn't it? If Clarissa had started talking about her three hundred dollar shoes one more time, I would have screamed."

My father chuckled. "I'm sorry you got stuck entertaining those two. It must have been quite a chore."

"That's okay," I assured him. I didn't want him to feel any worse than he was already feeling. In fact, I went over and gave him a big hug. "Don't worry, Daddy. Katherine and Elizabeth and I would never in a million years act like that awful Clarissa and her sister Bethany."

My father returned my hug. But when he pulled away, there was a serious look on his face. "I want to make sure of that, honey."

"What do you mean?"

"Sam, I think it's important that my daughters learn the value of money. Meeting Clarissa and Bethany got me thinking. Over dinner—actually, while trying to stomach that rich, sweet strawberry supreme whatever—I came up with an idea."

"Yes, Daddy?"

"Sam, I want you and Elizabeth to get jobs."

"Jobs?" I looked at him, blinking hard.

"That's right," he went on. "Katherine is still too

young, of course. She *is* only in the fifth grade. But I want you and Elizabeth to find out what it means to work, to go out into the world and earn your own money. It's not good to have everything come too easily. I think Ellsworth's daughters are proof of that.''

"I agree with you about Bethany and Clarissa, Daddy,'' I said, "but a *job*?''

"Exactly, Samantha. A job.''

I could tell by the firmness in his voice that even though I wasn't entirely crazy about this idea, my father was. There was no sense in arguing—unless, of course, I was prepared to lose.

"But . . . but what *kind* of job? What could I possibly do?'' In a meek voice, I added, "I *am* only twelve years old.''

"That's up to you, Sam,'' he said. Smiling, he added, "You're a smart cookie. You'll think of something.''

Suddenly his smile faded. "You know, there's a good reason why I invited Ellsworth von Thornbottom over here tonight in the first place. The truth of the matter is that I'm looking for additional investors for Langtree Industries.''

I gasped. "Daddy, is your company in trouble?''

His shoulders slumped a little. "I'm afraid so, sweetie. The computer business is always competitive, but lately things have been getting bad.''

"Maybe people have just stopped buying computers for a while,'' I suggested, trying to be helpful. "I'm sure things will pick up again soon.''

"It's more than that, Sam. It seems that every time

Langtree Industries starts developing a new product—something that looks really promising—one of our competitors beats us to the finish line.'' My father shook his head slowly. "It's happened a few times in the past six or eight months, and it's causing some real financial problems within the company. That's why I was hoping I could get Ellsworth interested in bailing us out. . . .''

"I know one thing we can do,'' I piped up. "You could stop giving us all a weekly allowance. I know I have more than enough money for the things I need, books and school supplies and milkshakes when I go out with my friends. There's plenty in my piggy bank upstairs, and of course there's the savings account at the bank that you and mom set up for me when I was a little girl. . . .''

My father was smiling. "Thank you, honey. But I don't think it's gotten to that point yet.''

"At any rate, Daddy, when I find a job, I'm going to give you every penny I make so you can pour it back into your company.''

"That's so sweet of you, Samantha,'' my father said. He came over to give me another hug. "But I don't want you worrying about me and my problems with my company.''

Of course, he hadn't taken my suggestion seriously. And it was true that the few dollars I could earn in my future job—whatever job that might turn out to be—would hardly make a dent in what his company needed.

Now that I was faced with the possibility that the Langtree family might have to cut back in some really serious ways, I was forced to think about how I really felt about it. And I could honestly say that it didn't bother me very much. While it was great being able to travel all over the world and live in a nice house and buy just about anything I wanted, I was old enough to realize that things like that took a backseat to the really important things in life, things like my wonderful family and my terrific friends.

But I could see how much it bothered my father. And one thing was certain. I wanted to help him get his company out of trouble. And no matter what it took, if there was anything I could do to help—anything at all—I was determined to do it.

chapter
two

"A *job* . . . do you believe it?" I wailed. "I mean, I love my father, but this time I really think he's gone off the deep end."

I was feeling pretty miserable as I dove into the bowl of pretzels that was keeping me, Betsy, and Carla company as we sat on the floor of Carla's bedroom that Friday night. It was almost exactly forty-eight hours after Daddy had come up with his brilliant idea, the one about it being time for his two older daughters to enter the working world.

"I don't think it's such a bad idea," Betsy said gently. She was hugging a pillow, one of the pink ones Carla usually keeps on her bed. Like me, she was wearing jeans and a comfortable sweater—just the thing for a weekend gabfest with friends. Betsy has this really great wild red hair—not that she thinks it's great, of course—that goes perfectly with her sparkly green eyes and the freckles scattered across her nose, like stars across a summer sky. The sweater she was wearing was a bright shade of green, the exact same shade as her eyes. Well, almost.

But it wasn't her cool hair or her terrific color sense that I was thinking about as I looked over at her, surprised.

"You don't think it's such a bad idea?" I repeated, barely able to believe I had heard her right.

"No, I don't," she replied matter-of-factly. "In fact, I think it could actually turn out to be a *good* idea."

"I agree with Betsy," Carla said. She was staring at the little pile of pretzels she had measured out on a paper napkin and set on the rug in front of her. As I've already mentioned, she's really committed to losing weight. She had just started a new diet, eating much more carefully and going for a long walk practically every day. And from her reports of her bathroom scale's readings, it was already beginning to pay off.

Not that I saw a chubby girl when I looked at her. To me, Carla Farrell just looked like a warm, caring person with a great sense of humor. At this point, I barely even noticed that she had short, curly brown hair and hazel eyes, much less that she was a little bit overweight. When I looked at her, I simply saw a friend.

"I think it could be kind of fun, getting a job," Carla went on. "You'd get to try something new, meet some new people, act a little bit more independent. . . . And then there's the money part. Don't forget about that."

"Carla's right." Betsy was nodding. "Those are all good reasons to see this idea of your dad's as a really *positive* thing. A challenge. A mission. A chance to get out there and prove yourself . . ."

"Okay, smarty-pants," I interrupted. "If you're both convinced that getting a job is the best thing since . . . since the invention of Velcro, maybe you'll be able to come up with some ideas."

"Ideas?" Carla said, blinking.

"That's right. *Ideas*. Ideas for what kind of job I can get. Keep in mind, of course, that I *am* only twelve years old."

I knew I had them. A long silence fell over the room. I couldn't help feeling just the teensiest bit smug.

I should have guessed that it wouldn't last very long. The one thing that the Bubble Gum Gang is good at is coming up with *brainstorms*. Especially where Betsy Crane, our number-one brain, is concerned.

"Let's see," she said. "You could get a paper route. You could hand out flyers for a store or some other business, either at the mall or on a busy street corner . . . or maybe go door to door in your neighborhood. You could start a dog-walking service—or a dog-*washing* service. You could bring people's bottles and newspapers to the recycling center to save them the trip. You could tutor elementary school kids in the subjects they're having trouble with. You could—"

"Stop!" I cried, holding my hands up to my ears. "Enough!"

"I think what Betsy is saying," Carla said calmly,

"is that there are really a lot of things you could do, if you just spend a little time thinking about it."

"Exactly my point," Betsy agreed. "It's simply a question of doing some creative thinking and then picking out what's best for you."

"Okay," I muttered, running through her list in my mind. "Dog washing? I don't think so. I don't have a tub that's big enough, and my mother would never let me use any of the bathrooms to wash other people's animals. Dog walking? A possibility, although with winter just around the corner . . ."

"There's always baby-sitting." Carla popped a pretzel into her mouth. They were the no-salt kind—much healthier than the salted kind, she had informed us.

"Baby-sitting?" I squealed. "I don't know a *thing* about baby-sitting."

"It's not very hard," Betsy said. "In fact, it can actually be kind of fun."

"Fun?" I knew I was beginning to sound like an echo, but I couldn't help myself.

"Sure," Betsy replied. "Easy, too. There's a zillion ways of keeping little kids occupied. You can read them stories. They always like that."

"Or do art projects with them," Carla added, growing excited. "That's always been the part I liked best. You can make things out of clay. . . ."

"Or papier-mâché," Betsy said. "That is, if they're old enough."

"You can paint. . . ."

"Finger paints!"

"And there's always the old standby: making things

out of construction paper, scissors, paste, stick-ers. . . .''

''And there are other things you can do, too. I've always enjoyed taking little kids to the playground.'' Betsy was wearing a big grin. ''Pushing them on the swings, cheering them on as they went down the slide . . . I even used to enjoy taking my little brother Brad to the park, and he's only three years younger than I am.''

''All right, you two. I get the idea.'' I sighed. ''You've almost got me convinced that baby-sitting is the way to go.''

'' 'Almost?' '' Betsy teased. ''What do you mean, 'almost'?''

''Well . . . I still haven't figured out who I could baby-sit for.''

Carla was nodding thoughtfully. ''Good point, Sam. But even that shouldn't be too hard. You could advertise in the local newspaper.''

''Or make up a little flyer and leave it in people's mailboxes. If I were you, I'd look for houses with swing sets in the backyard.''

''Wait a minute! I have an even better idea,'' I cried. ''I'll ask my father to put up a sign on the bulletin board at his office. There must be lots of employees at Langtree Industries who need a baby-sitter.

''Besides,'' I added, still not completely sure about this, ''my earning some money was his idea in the first place. I want him to know that I'm serious about giving it my best shot.''

Betsy and Carla agreed that this was an excellent

plan. Right then and there, they helped me make up two posters offering my services as a baby-sitter. They told me exactly what to put on the posters, reminding me to include what days and hours I was available, how much I charged, and where I could be reached by phone.

"There!" I exclaimed, admiring our handiwork: two yellow cardboard signs, neatly hand lettered with black marker. "Thanks. We did a great job."

"Not bad, if I do say so myself." All of a sudden, Betsy grew serious. "Okay, Sam. I think that now it's time for me and Carla to tell you about the *other* side of baby-sitting."

"The other side?" This didn't sound good.

"I think what Betsy means," Carla said slowly, "is that all kids are not exactly angels."

"That's an understatement," Betsy cried. "I once had a little girl pour a whole bottle of glue on my head!"

"I once had a little boy sneak into the kitchen while I was busy playing Uncle Wiggly with his two sisters upstairs in their bedroom. He ate an entire half gallon of chocolate ice cream." Carla rolled her eyes. "He was sick for three days. And boy, was his mother mad at me!"

"That's nothing," Betsy said. "What about the time a set of twins I was sitting for decided to surprise their parents by painting pictures all over the hallway? Talk about an angry mother!"

"Paint? Ice cream? Glue?" I gulped. "Why didn't you two tell me about any of this before?"

"Oh, it's not always like that," Betsy assured me.

"Right," Carla said. "Only some of the time. We just want to make sure you're going into this with all the facts."

"My advice is to be prepared," Betsy said. "Bring plenty of things for the kids to do. Books to read to them, for example. You can get those out of the library."

"Or even old magazines and catalogues," Carla suggested. "Kids love to cut out pictures." She thought for a moment. "*My* advice is, don't ever take your eyes off the kids you're baby-sitting, not even for an instant."

"I get it," I said, my voice cracking. "Otherwise you might end up with painted hallways and sticky hair. And empty cartons of ice cream."

"Relax, Sam. Don't worry about it," Betsy reassured me. "You'll do fine. You're creative. You're energetic. And most important, you're good at thinking on your feet."

"Betsy's absolutely right," Carla said. "Besides, you've got one more advantage."

"What's that?" I asked in a meek voice.

"Chances are, you'll be bigger than they are."

As I was letting out a low moan, Betsy said, "You'll make a great baby-sitter, Sam. I promise."

"Just make sure you don't work every night of every weekend," Carla said. "One of these days, I'm going to be inviting you to something special."

"What do you mean?"

"Actually, it was my parents' idea. They're so thrilled that I'm on this diet that they promised me a frozen yogurt party at Yo-Yo's Yogurt as a reward for losing my next five pounds—whenever that is.'' She popped the last of the pretzels into her mouth. ''The way things are going so far, I have a feeling it won't be long at all.''

''I'd love to help you celebrate having lost five pounds,'' Betsy said. ''And eating yummy frozen yogurt—low fat, low calorie—is a great way to do it.''

''Count me in, too,'' I said.

Carla was beaming. ''Thanks, you two. It means a lot to me that you're both cheering me on during this diet.''

''Gee, Carla. We know how important it is to you.'' Suddenly Betsy snapped her fingers. ''I know. The night of the frozen yogurt party, let's all get really dressed up. We'll make it a real occasion. We can put on our best clothes, fix our hair in a special way—''

''Hair!'' I cried. ''That reminds me.''

I reached for the tote bag I had brought along that evening. Actually, it was a shopping bag from Harrod's, the fanciest department store in London. Dramatically I dumped it out onto the rug, right smack in the middle of the little circle we three Bubble Gum Gang members had formed.

''Look at all the hair stuff,'' Carla exclaimed. ''Wow! Ribbons, headbands, barrettes, clips . . .''

''Even those scrunchy things you can wear around your ponytail. Sam, you'd look great in that blue one.''

''Help yourselves,'' I offered. ''We have a whole carton of them at home. This is just a drop in the bucket.''

''Where did you get them?'' asked Betsy, fastening

a purple barrette into her hair. I had to admit, it looked terrific with her red curls.

"An old friend of my father's came over for dinner a couple of nights ago. He just bought the company that manufactures them, and he brought all these as a present."

"That was nice of him," Carla said, picking through the collection of brightly colored hair ornaments strewn about the carpet.

"I think he was partly showing off," I told them, laughing. "But that's okay. We can still have a great time wearing them. Here, Carla, try this one. It'll look dynamite on you, with your coloring."

For the rest of the evening, we forgot all about serious stuff like getting jobs and dieting. We had a blast, the three of us, putting on all the barrettes and headbands and everything else, trying out a million different hairstyles.

This, after all, was really what being in the Bubble Gum Gang was all about. And it was what Friday nights were all about, too. Hanging out. Being with friends. And just having plain, old-fashioned fun.

chapter
three

Given the exciting new development in my life—
that I was about to enter the challenging and mysterious world of baby-sitting—I quickly forgot about
Ellsworth von Thornbottom's hair ornaments. It was
my father who reminded me, right after I told him
about my idea of having him advertise my services at
his company.

"Put up posters at my office?" he repeated uncer-
tainly over breakfast on Monday morning. I had just
shown him the beautiful hand-lettered signs we had
made at Carla's house. I was convinced that their professional appearance would help cancel out any doubts
he might have about the idea.

"Why not?" my mother asked. "Bill, I think that's
a fine idea. Somebody at your office is bound to need
a baby-sitter. Samantha, that was very clever of you."

Beaming, I turned back to my father. "Well, Dad?
Will you do it? Please?"

"Well . . . all right." And then he melted. "It *was*
clever of you, Samantha. I'm proud of you for taking

all this so seriously. And I appreciate the way you got right on it.''

"I'm working on getting a job, too," Elizabeth piped up. "I'm going to give piano lessons. I thought I'd put up a sign at the music store in town, and another at the library.''

"That's a lovely idea," Mother said. "Goodness, Bill, what creative, hardworking daughters we have.''

"I wish I could get a job," Katherine mumbled into her glass of orange juice.

"That time will come soon enough," my mother assured her. "For now, your job is to work as hard as you can at your schoolwork.''

"By the way," Dad said, gesturing toward the box of hair ornaments sitting on the windowsill in the dining room, where we were eating, "let's not forget Ellsworth's thoughtful gift. We really should find some way of using all those hair thingamabobs.''

Elizabeth giggled. "I know. Maybe we could sell them door to door." She crunched on a piece of cinnamon toast. "You know, the way the Girl Scouts sell cookies.''

"Or we could have a yard sale," Katherine said. "I've always wanted to do that.''

"All of a sudden, everybody around here wants to go into business," my father teased. "I appreciate how ambitious you all are. But in the meantime, how about each of you bringing some to school? You could give them out to your friends, your teachers, whoever wants them.''

"I'll do my part," I volunteered. I made a quick stop in the kitchen, stuffed two or three dozen hair ornaments into a paper bag, picked up my school-books, and was off.

But of course, I had already given a bunch of hair ornaments to my best friends, Carla and Betsy. Frankly, I didn't know what I was going to do with this fresh batch.

"Maybe I'll just pass the bag around my first-period English class," I muttered to myself as I walked up the front steps and into the school building.

Hanover Junior High might have been here in the good old U.S.A., rather than in Switzerland, and its name might have been in English instead of French, but it was still *my* school . . . and I was perfectly satisfied going there. Unlike *some* people, of course . . .

Thinking about Bethany and Clarissa again suddenly made me feel as if I wanted no part of them or their parents—or their silly hair ornaments. The paper bag in my hand was already beginning to seem like a burden. I just wanted to unload all that hair stuff. And the faster, the better.

I was still busy thinking about the hair ornaments as I went inside the school building. Walking down the corridor just a few feet in front of me, I noticed, were Wendy Lipton and Kicky Blake.

I think I'd better take a moment to explain something about Wendy and Kicky. They're the ringleaders of the clique of girls who run just about everything at our school—and have always taken great pleasure in excluding everybody else, me included. Both of them are cheerleaders. Wendy, in fact, is head cheerleader. She also tried out for the same part as Carla in the school play . . . but that was another episode in the life of the Bubble Gum Gang.

Basically, Wendy and Kicky are pretty, they're popular, and they have the trendiest clothes—at least, by Hanover Junior High School's standards. Compared to what they're wearing in Paris these days, those two are ages behind. But they would never give a hoot about something like that. Their world extends no further than Hanover, and their lives consist of nothing more than catching the eye of the cutest boys, giving the coolest parties, and just generally trying to be the center of attention.

Today was no exception.

"Wendy, will you *look* at me?" Kicky was squealing. "I'm such a *mess* today!"

If I thought I looked like a mess, I was thinking, I certainly wouldn't go around pointing it out to everybody.

"I can't believe my alarm clock didn't go off," she went on, moaning. "And here I had planned to wash my hair—which is *so* icky—before I dared set foot in school. But instead of getting up at seven, the way I'd planned, I didn't get up until eight, when my mother woke me up. Will you just look at my hair? Oh, no— don't. Please, don't look!"

As far as I could tell, Kicky's hair looked fine. In fact, it looked exactly the way it always looked. She has long, thick, jet black hair, and she usually wears it either just hanging down or in a ponytail.

I don't know what came over me. There's no way I can explain it. But all of a sudden, I found myself walking right up to Kicky—Kicky, who had never once said a friendly word to me, ever since the third grade when I first met her, who has made a sort of career out of teasing me, calling me "snob" and "poor little rich girl." I stood in front of her, held out my paper bag, and said, in this really nice, cheerful voice, "Here, Kicky. Maybe you'd like one of these."

For a few endlessly long seconds, Kicky just stared at me. It was as if she simply could not believe that Samantha Langtree was actually daring to speak to her. But in the end, her curiosity got the best of her. Or, to be more accurate, *Wendy's* curiosity got the best of *her*.

"What's this?" Wendy demanded, poking her nose inside the bag. "Your lunch?"

"No, of course it's not my lunch," I replied tartly. "They're hair ornaments. Twenty or thirty, at least. Since you're worried about how your hair looks, Kicky, I thought you might like to have one."

Now Kicky peered inside the bag. "Look at all the hair stuff!" she cried. "Gee, a red velvet headband, trimmed with gold. I've always wanted one of those. And tortoise-shell clips . . . and those are really cool barrettes."

"The second I heard you complaining about your hair," I said matter-of-factly, "I wanted you to have one."

"Really? Wow. Can I take . . . a few of them?"

"Sure. In fact, take them all."

"*All* of them?"

"Why not? In fact, you'd be doing me a favor. I really want to help them find a good home, but to be perfectly honest, I'm not really crazy about the idea of spending my entire day trying to find girls who want them. How about if you two divide them up? Or give them out to some of your other friends. Whatever you want to do is fine with me.''

Kicky looked at Wendy, her eyes still wide with disbelief. And then, in one quick motion, she reached over and snatched the bag from my hand.

''Thanks, Samantha,'' she said, still looking amazed. And then, suddenly, the expression on her face softened. ''You know, this is very nice of you.''

I shrugged. ''I'm just glad to have found somebody who can use them. Besides, it's not as if I didn't have even more at home.''

''You have more?'' Wendy asked.

''Sure. You see, what happened was this friend of my father's brought over a huge carton of them the other night. More than we could ever use ourselves, even with three daughters and a mother in the house. This friend of Dad's just bought the company that manufactures them.''

''He owns the company?'' Kicky breathed. ''Boy, my parents sure don't have such interesting friends. And they certainly don't have any friends who give out presents like these.''

Just then, the warning bell rang, the one that meant we had only five minutes to get to our lockers and then to homeroom.

''Well, gee, Samantha,'' Kicky said, wearing a big, friendly smile, ''I guess I'd better rush off to the girls' room to do something with this mop of mine. But, uh, thanks again.''

"Any time, Kicky." Already I was turning around, heading toward my locker.

"Yeah, thanks, Samantha," Wendy called after me, still sounding a little surprised.

I must admit, she wasn't the only one who was feeling surprised.

Maybe Kicky and Wendy aren't so bad, after all, I was thinking as I walked away. Wouldn't *that* turn out to be the shock of a lifetime.

"What do you *mean*, Wendy and Kicky might not be so bad after all?" yelped Carla.

It was right after school, and the three of us had just settled in at my house. We were sitting in the den, munching apples. All in all, it felt kind of like a special occasion. Now that Carla was involved with the Drama Club, she had to stay after school for rehearsals for *Our Town* most days. Today was one of those days she was free to join Betsy and me for some serious hanging out.

Yet the moment I introduced the subject of Wendy Lipton and Kicky Blake, the mood changed. Betsy's and Carla's eyes were boring into me. I started squirming around on our white leather couch, suddenly feeling extremely uncomfortable.

"Well . . ." I said, "all I meant was, maybe I've been misjudging the two of them all these years."

"Samantha Langtree!" Carla cried. "Betsy may be new to this town, but I'm not. I've known Kicky and Wendy ever since I was five years old. And believe me, even back in kindergarten they were nothing but trouble. I remember this one time, Wendy spilled her apple juice all over me during snack time, and when the teacher came over to ask who spilled it, she blamed it on *me*! And then there was the time Wendy and Kicky took all the crayons out of my cubby and hid them in the blankets we had all brought up for rest period—"

"But Carla," I broke in, "all of that happened seven years ago."

Betsy rushed to her aid. "Samantha," she said coldly, "surely you're not forgetting that Carla and Wendy were rivals for the part of Emily in the school production of *Our Town*?"

"Of course I haven't forgotten, but that doesn't mean—"

"So my question is," Betsy went on, "where is your sense of loyalty?"

"Wait a minute. Hold on here." I held up my hands, pleading with them both to stop. Frankly, I was surprised by their reaction. All I had said was that earlier that day, when I had offered some of the hair ornaments to Wendy and Kicky, they had seemed very grateful. I mentioned that they were actually sort of friendly toward me.

From Betsy and Carla's reaction, you would have thought I had invited Kicky and Wendy to join the Bubble Gum Gang.

I must admit, I was a little bit shaken up. After all, this was the first time there had been a major disagreement within the group. Oh, sure, there had been heated discussions about which video to rent for the evening. And then there was the time we got into quite a debate about who was the cutest actor in Hollywood.

But this was much more personal. And it had much more potential to get blown up all out of proportion.

"Look," I said, not wanting to show how exasperated I was. "All I'm saying is that I found out today that Wendy and Kicky have another side to them. They can be nice, normal, friendly girls. Believe me, I'm just as surprised as you are."

"Hmph," Carla sniffed. "Just don't say Betsy and I didn't warn you."

That remark really caught me off guard. "Warn me about what?"

"I think what Carla means," Betsy said, "is that it seems like more than just a coincidence that the one time in their lives that Kicky and Wendy are nice to you is when you've just given them a whole bag of free hair ornaments."

I blinked. "Do you really think you're being fair?"

Betsy and Carla just looked at each other. I could see I wasn't the only one who was getting exasperated.

"Just be careful," Betsy said, looking at me meaningfully.

I was just about to open my mouth to ask her what I should be careful *of* when the telephone rang. Since there's a phone right in the den, I jumped up and grabbed it before the first ring was even finished.

"Hello?" I asked, expecting it to be one of Elizabeth's friends, or maybe one of Katherine's.

Instead, I heard a deep male voice ask, "Hello, may I please speak to Samantha?"

"This is Samantha," I replied. I must admit, I was pretty confused.

"I'm an executive at Langtree Industries, and today I saw your sign on the bulletin board. The one advertising baby-sitting services."

All of a sudden, everything clicked into place. I put on my most responsible, most grown-up voice.

"Why, yes," I said. "That's me. I mean, I'm the baby-sitter. I mean . . ."

As soon as my two pals figured out what this telephone call was all about, they began jumping around excitedly.

"Go for it!" Carla cried. She held up both hands. All her fingers were crossed.

Meanwhile, the man was asking, "How does the idea of sitting for three children strike you?"

"Three children?" I repeated. My face must have reflected my horror. But Betsy and Carla were nodding at me.

"Say yes! Say yes!" Carla was whispering.

"Uh, no problem," I assured the man. Somehow, I actually managed to sound as if I meant it.

"Fine! Any chance you'll be free this Wednesday evening?"

"Wednesday evening?" I glanced at Carla and Betsy. They were nodding furiously. "Wednesday evening sounds fine."

"Well, then, what do you say we give it a try? My wife and I have plans to go out to dinner, so we'll only be out from, say, seven o'clock until ten. Is that too late for a school night?"

This time, I didn't even bother to check with my

cheering squad. "No, not at all. Seven to ten is perfect."

"Good. Then I'll give you my name and address. Got a pen?"

Betsy had already produced one.

"Shoot."

"My name is Steve McArdle, and I live in Hanover. The address is Thirty-seven Oak Court."

"Got it. Steve McArdle, Thirty-seven Oak Court, seven o'clock sharp."

"And what is your last name, please?"

"Oh, I guess I forgot to mention that, didn't I?" This baby-sitting business was already turning out to be trickier than I had expected. "My last name is Langtree."

There was a long silence at the other end of the line. "Langtree?" Mr. McArdle finally repeated. "As in Bill Langtree, president of Langtree Industries—in other words, my boss?"

"That's me," I informed him cheerfully. I could see the looks of panic on Carla's and Betsy's faces. "Uh, that's not a problem, is it?"

"No, no, not at all," he was quick to assure me. "It's just . . . I was caught off guard a bit. I never expected my boss's daughter to end up becoming my baby-sitter."

"Well, Mr. McArdle, to tell you the truth, I never exactly expected to become a baby-sitter, either."

"Excuse me?"

"See you this Wednesday at seven," I chirped, and I hung up.

"You did it!" cried Betsy.

''You're a real, official baby-sitter!'' Carla was jumping up and down, clapping her hands.

I just sat there, grinning from ear to ear. ''I *did* do it, didn't I? I really did. I went out and got myself a job. I am now officially part of the working world!''

I was so excited about how quickly everything had fallen into place that it never occurred to me, not even for a second, that the hardest part was yet to come.

chapter
four

As I stood on the McArdles' doorstep at five minutes to seven the following Wednesday night, I was as excited as if I were going to a wonderful party. I was nervous, too, as I rang the bell of what had turned out to be a large, luxurious house, the fanciest one on the block. In the backyard, I could see, there was a huge swing set and a jungle gym, the kind you usually see at public playgrounds. They even had a tree house back there. And there were toys everywhere: bicycles, basketballs, roller skates, wagons.

I thought I was ready for anything. I had brought along a few games I had enjoyed as a child, a little dusty from being stashed in the basement but more or less with all their pieces. I had gone to the library after school and checked out half a dozen picture books. I'd even brought art supplies, a whole shoebox full of crayons and markers and pipe cleaners. All in all, I had done a thorough job, taking to heart all the good advice Carla and Betsy had given me.

I *thought* I was ready for anything . . . until Ms. McArdle threw open the front door.

I barely saw her smiling face. I hardly heard her say, "Hello. You must be Samantha." I didn't even notice that she was all dressed up, obviously on her way out to some grand occasion.

I was too astonished by what was going on *behind* her.

The scene in the living room was about as close as you can get to a three-ring circus without sitting in a tent. Each one of the three McArdle children was on a rampage—or so it seemed as I stood there, open-mouthed.

A little girl about five years old, her long brown hair a disheveled mess, was stomping through the living room, dressed in a pair of rubber boots, a fur jacket twenty sizes too big for her, and an expensive-looking man's hat. She was singing at the top of her lungs. Meanwhile, a little boy with brown hair and a devilish grin, a year or two older, was climbing all over the couch, acting as if *this* was his jungle gym, not the contraption out back. A baby, no more than two, was sitting on the floor, happily smearing grape jelly all over that evening's newspaper.

A box of cookies had been overturned, and ginger snaps were strewn all over the rug. The television was on full blast. So was the radio.

"Oh, these children!" Ms. McArdle cried, suddenly looking sheepish. It was as if she finally figured out that I was looking right past her, at the wild scene inside the living room. "They're so . . . energetic. Sometimes I don't know *what* to do with them." She let out a high-pitched giggle. "But I suppose you already know how children are."

Nervously I cleared my throat. "To tell you the truth, Ms. McArdle, I *don't*. You see, I've never actually baby-sat before."

"You haven't?"

I shook my head.

Ms. McArdle thought for a moment. "Oh. Well, I'm sure you'll do fine, once you get into the swing of things." She was talking in a very chirpy voice. "Now, how about if I introduce you to the children?"

I just nodded. At that point, I don't think I could have managed to get any words out if my life depended on it.

"Jimmy, Patty, I'd like you to meet your new baby-sitter," Ms. McArdle yelled above the noise. I wasn't surprised that she got very little response.

She didn't seem very surprised, either. Finally she walked over to the television and snapped it off. The radio was next.

"Hey, I was watching that!" shrieked the oldest child, seven-year-old Jimmy. At the moment, he was balancing on the back of the couch like a tightrope walker.

"Jimmy, I want you to come off there right now! This is Samantha, your new baby-sitter."

"Samantha?" the boy repeated. "What kind of name is *that*?"

"You can call me Sam, if you like." I forced myself to smile. "All my friends do." Meanwhile, I was wondering if it was too late to back out of this without my father thinking I was a quitter.

But Ms. McArdle was acting as if everything was just fine.

"And this is Patty. She's five. Patty, honey, I really don't like you wearing my mink jacket."

The little girl just stared at her.

"Well, just be careful with it, okay?" Ms. McArdle said. "It cost a lot of money. It's not a toy."

Already she had turned her attention to the baby.

"And this is Willy. He's two." Meaningfully, she added, "You really have to watch him, Samantha. He's at an age where he gets into everything." She placed a little kiss on top of his golden head. He barely looked up from finger painting the newspaper with the jelly.

Carla, Betsy . . . where are you now that I need you? I was thinking. I felt desperate. I felt panicked. I felt like this was going to be the worst evening of my entire life.

And I felt like there was absolutely nothing I could do about it.

"We're going to be leaving in a minute or two—oh, here's my husband now." Ms. McArdle was beaming as a man all dressed up in a suit—Mr. McArdle, no doubt—came down the stairs and into the living room.

"Hello, Samantha," he said cheerfully. He walked over and shook my hand. Ordinarily, that would have made me feel very grown-up. At the moment, however, grown-up was the last thing I wanted to be. "It's so nice to meet you. I'm sure you'll have no problem tonight. You look like a mature, responsible young woman."

I opened my mouth to protest, to ask the McArdles if they were really, really sure they felt safe leaving their three little darlings in the care of someone who secretly wanted nothing more than to dash out of there as fast as she could. But they were already going over to the closet and taking out their coats.

"The children haven't had their dinner yet," Ms. McArdle called over to me. "There's a package of hot dogs in the refrigerator, and some French fries you can heat up in the microwave. And I believe you'll find some carrots in there, too. See if you can get the kids to eat *something* that's good for them."

She gave me a weak smile. "They'll need baths, and I'd like them in bed no later than eight-thirty. Willy should get to bed earlier, I suppose, but he pretty much does whatever his big brother and sister do."

"Uh, Ms. McArdle? Is there a telephone number where I can reach you? If there's any problem, I mean."

Mr. and Ms. McArdle looked at each other.

"I suppose I could give you the name of the restaurant where we're going," Mr. McArdle said. He jotted down a name and number on a scrap of paper and handed it to me. "But this is a pretty important occasion, so please don't call us unless there's a real emergency."

When they were gone, I closed my eyes, took a few deep breaths, and walked into the living room.

"Hello, Jimmy," I said politely. "Uh, what grade are you in?"

Jimmy just glanced at me, then went back to staring at the cartoons that were on television.

"You certainly have a lot of toys," I said, trying to sound enthusiastic and interested.

Once again, he ignored me.

"So, uh, do your mommy and daddy go out a lot?"

"All the time," Jimmy replied. His eyes never left the screen. "Practically every night."

"Oh! When do you get to see them?"

Jimmy shrugged. "We spend a lot of time with baby-sitters. Hey, can I stay up to watch extra television? There's this cool movie on at nine. It's called *Return of the Killer Ninja Aliens*."

"No. Absolutely not!"

The little boy looked over at me, astonished. "What do you mean, no?"

"I said no, Jimmy. First of all, you can't stay up extra late. Second, that doesn't sound like the kind of movie your parents would allow a seven-year-old boy to watch."

"Aw, they don't care what I watch," he muttered. "My baby-sitters don't care, either."

"Well, *I* care, Jimmy," I said. But he was already absorbed in his cartoons.

I decided to give Patty a try. She had given up on parading around in her mother's fur jacket. Instead, she was draped across a chair, looking bored as she watched her baby brother.

"So you're five years old, aren't you?" I said to Patty. I crouched down next to Willy and gently took the grape jelly away from him. At first he started to wail, but I quickly handed him the colorful plastic rattle I had spotted under the coffee table. That seemed to interest him almost as much as painting great masterpieces with food.

Patty was busy watching me with Willy. "What are you doing?"

"I'm taking the jelly away from him. That's not the way a two-year-old should be playing." I couldn't resist adding, "Don't your parents get upset when he does things like that?"

Patty shook her head. "No. My mom just says what she always says, that she can't keep up with us kids."

"And your daddy?"

"He's never home. He's always at work."

I crumpled up the purple newspaper to throw it away. "Well, it's getting to be dinner time. I still have to give each of you a bath—"

"I don't want dinner. And I don't want a bath."

"You don't want dinner? Aren't you hungry, Patty?"

"A little." The little girl's face lit up. "Can I have an ice cream cone for dinner?"

"No, Patty, you can't."

"Why not?" she pouted.

"Hey, I want ice cream for dinner, too," Jimmy said. "There's chocolate ice cream in the freezer. I want some."

"Ice cream! Ice cream!" Patty began chanting.

It wasn't long before Jimmy joined in. Willy, too, was screeching, "Eye cream! Eye cream!" as loudly as he could.

Suddenly I couldn't take any more.

"Okay, you little monsters," I hissed. I stood up, stalked over to the television, and snapped it off.

"We're going to lay some ground rules around here—and I don't want to hear a peep out of any of you!"

Three pairs of eyes just stared at me in amazement. But not one of the three McArdle children said a word. For the first time since I'd rung the doorbell, I felt like I was in control.

"All right. Here's the deal. First we're all going to go into the kitchen. While I'm making you dinner, you're going to sit at the kitchen table and color."

"I *hate* coloring," Jimmy whined. But one sharp look in his direction and that was the end of that.

"Then, you're all going to eat your dinner. All of it. Hot dogs, French fries, and carrots."

"I *hate* carrots," cried Patty.

"If you don't eat your carrots, there won't be any story before bed."

"Story before bed?" Jimmy repeated. "Nobody ever reads us a story before bed."

"Well, I read stories before bed. And the kids are allowed to pick out the books they want. I brought six of them, and you can each choose one. That is, *if* you behave from now until then."

"What else do we have to do?" Patty asked. She was looking at me in this funny way, as if she wasn't sure what to make of all this.

"After you eat all your dinner, you each have to take a bath. And that means no splashing and no clowning around. Five minutes in the tub and then out."

"Can we have bubbles?" Patty asked shyly.

"Yes, you can have bubbles. And then, you get your story. *After* you have your pajamas on and you're in bed.'' I looked from Jimmy to Patty and back to Jimmy. "Okay. Any questions?"

I wish I could report that the rest of the evening went smoothly. I wish I could say that Jimmy and Patty and Willy ate all their dinner, even their carrots. That no bubbles ended up on the ceiling of the McArdles' bathroom. And that I got them to put on their pajamas without chasing them around the house, all of us screaming like wild animals.

But the truth is, the rest of the evening went almost as badly as the first part. It was a struggle every step of the way. Nothing that Carla and Betsy had said had prepared me for *this*.

Finally, at eight forty-five, Willy was asleep on the floor of his room, Patty was curled up in her bed, humming to herself, and Jimmy was sitting at the edge, looking through the books I had brought. Sure, they were all clean, and they each had at least some food in their stomachs.

But the bathroom looked like a hurricane had come through it, complete with flooding and almost total destruction. The kitchen looked kind of like that, too. There were more carrots on the floor than I had gotten into all three of the children combined. Everything else was a mess, too. There were clothes and toys everywhere, and a big fat smear of toothpaste now decorated Patty's dresser. Needless to say, I was completely exhausted.

"This is the book I want," Jimmy finally said, handing me a copy of *The Little Engine That Could*.

I just looked at him. "Excuse me?"

"You said you'd read us a story when it was time for bed."

"That's right," Patty said, jumping out of bed. "I want to choose my book. Oooh, is that one about bunnies? I see a picture of bunnies on the cover."

"Wait just a minute," I cried. "What I said was that I would read each of you a book *if* you behaved all evening. Now, really, do you think you behaved this evening?"

Jimmy and Patty just looked at me, confused.

"We acted the way we always act," Jimmy finally said.

"Give me a break, Jimmy," I told him. "Tell me honestly. Is this the way you act in school?"

His eyes grew round. "Are you kidding? My teacher would never let me get away with this stuff!"

"Well, Jimmy, I don't let kids get away with this stuff, either. And as far as I'm concerned, you two were total monsters this entire evening. You didn't hold up your end of the deal, and so I'm not going to, either."

"You're not going to read to us?" Patty said. She looked as if she were going to burst into tears.

But I held firm. "No, I'm not. Our deal was that reading stories was your reward for behaving."

I must admit, I felt kind of sorry for her. She really did look disappointed. But one glance at the toothpaste on her dresser took care of any feelings of regret I might have had.

Patty and Jimmy were quiet for a long time. And then, in this really quiet voice, Jimmy said, "Hey, Sam?"

"Yes, Jimmy?"

"Do you think that maybe if we behave better the next time you baby-sit for us, you might read us books at bedtime?"

"*Next time?*" I repeated, collapsing against the bed in exhaustion.

By the time Mr. and Ms. McArdle came home, I had done a halfway decent job of cleaning up. I didn't intend to make the place spic and span, since it was hardly that way when I first got there. But I wiped away the toothpaste, swatted the bubbles off the bathroom ceiling with a towel, and got most of the carrots off the kitchen floor. I was lying on the couch in a lifeless heap when they walked in.

"How did it go?" Ms. McArdle asked brightly. "I hope they didn't give you a hard time."

I jumped off the couch and stood facing her. "Ms. McArdle, the kids ate about an eighth of their carrots, they got water and bubbles all over the bathroom, and they didn't get to sleep until almost nine o'clock."

"Oh, good," she replied, looking relieved. "I'm so glad it went well!" She glanced around the living room. Beaming, she said, "My goodness. I see you straightened up, too."

"Ms. McArdle—" I protested.

"Well, now, Samantha, I can see you did a fine job, just as I expected you would," Mr. McArdle boomed. "You can be sure I'll mention this to your father. I must say, you've turned out to be one of the best baby-sitters we've ever had."

"Oh, yes," Ms. McArdle cooed. "Tell me, when

can you come back? Are you by any chance available this weekend?''

I stood there, amazed.

''That's right,'' Mr. McArdle was saying. ''We have that dinner party at the Stones' on Saturday night, don't we? We'll be out until after midnight. Are you free, by any chance?''

''Mr. McArdle—''

''If you'd like, I could ask your father about it,'' he went on, looking concerned. ''That is, if you're afraid he won't let you stay out that late.''

My *father*! The last thing in the world I wanted was for him to think I couldn't handle a simple baby-sitting job—even though that happened to be the truth. I was trapped. There was no way out.

''Saturday night?'' I croaked. ''Uh, what time do you need me?''

So there it was. I was going to be the McArdles' baby-sitter, even if it killed me. And from the way I felt, it looked as if that were a very strong possibility.

chapter
five

"Home," I muttered as I shuffled into my house late that night. My feet felt like two bundles of wet diapers, and my brain was as muddled as if there were soap bubbles on the ceiling of my head.

"Bed," I moaned. "I want my bed!"

I had just thrown myself across the bed in question when the telephone on the night table right next to it rang.

"Go away," I said into my pillow. But the ringing wouldn't stop.

Finally, I picked it up.

"Hello?"

I figured it was probably Betsy, or maybe Carla, calling for a report on my introduction to the wild world of baby-sitting. So I was surprised to hear a voice I didn't recognize.

"Hello, Samantha?" the girl at the other end of the wire said sweetly. "I hope I'm not calling too late. . . ."

"No, it's okay. Uh, who is this?"

"Oh, I'm sorry, Samantha." She giggled. "This is Kicky."

"Kicky?" I was wondering if in my exhausted state I was hearing things.

"How are you, Samantha?"

"Um, fine." I was still bewildered. Why on earth would Kicky Blake be calling me?

I got part of the answer right away.

"One of the reasons I'm calling is to thank you again for all that cool hair stuff you gave me the other day. As a matter of fact, I'm wearing the purple and green barrette right now. It goes great with the sweater I have on."

Was *that* all. "You're welcome, Kicky. It really was no big deal."

"But there's another reason I'm calling." Kicky took a deep breath. "This Friday night, a few of my friends are coming over. We've having what we call a 'make-over night.' We all get together and put on makeup and try different hairstyles. . . . Sometimes we even trade clothes. The whole thing is lots of fun."

"Oh, really?" To tell you the truth, I couldn't figure out why on earth she was telling me all this.

"It's just the usual crowd. Wendy Lipton is coming, of course. She *is* my best friend. And Jennifer Wills and Bobbi Carter will probably be there, too."

Jennifer Wills had been in my fifth-grade class. Not that she had paid any attention to me since then. Jennifer, like Wendy and Kicky, was a cheerleader. She was also a leading member of their crowd. Bobbi Carter was in that crowd, too, although I hardly knew her. What I did know was that overall, my impression of Jennifer and Bobbi was pretty much the same as the one I'd always had of Wendy and Kicky.

"Anyway," Kicky went on, "the reason I'm calling is to invite you to join us."

I nearly dropped the phone. Was it really possible that Kicky Blake, one of the most popular girls at school, was inviting me over to her house? Could it really be that the ringleaders of the school were interested in Samantha Langtree? Was it possible that, suddenly, they had started seeing me in a different light . . . and wanted to be friends with *me*?

Not only was it possible, it was actually happening.

And being surprised was only part of my reaction. I was also very, very flattered.

"To your house?" I repeated, still not sure I had heard this whole thing correctly.

"That's right. This Friday night, around seven."

"Well, I, uh . . ." I swallowed hard. "Sure, Kicky. That sounds great."

"Oh, good!" She sounded genuinely pleased. "You know where I live, don't you?"

"Near the park, right?"

"You've got it. It's Two-twenty-two Acorn Street." She hesitated. "Uh, Samantha? There's one more thing. Do you, uh, think you could bring some more of those hair ornaments? You did say you had a whole box of them, and just this morning Wendy and I were telling Jennifer and Bobbi all about how terrific they were. . . ."

"I'm sorry, Kicky, but they're all gone."

"Gone?"

"Yes. When I came home from school this afternoon, my little sister told me that she'd taken the rest of them to school. Katherine said the other fifth-grade girls pounced on them as if they were gold.''

I laughed. Kicky, I noticed, wasn't laughing.

''Oh. Gee, Samantha, I'm so disappointed. And I know Jennifer and Bobbi are going to be disappointed, too. You see, the way these make-over nights of ours always go is that everybody brings something for the group. You know, the person whose house it is is in charge of snacks, somebody else brings an exercise video or one on hairstyling or professional makeup techniques. . . . Anyway, I was thinking that what you could bring was more hair stuff.''

I could sense her disappointment. And suddenly, all I wanted to do was make it go away. Here I was coming so close to being accepted to the most exclusive group of girls at our school. I wasn't about to let an opportunity like that slip through my fingers.

''I'll tell you what,'' I offered. ''How about if, instead, I bring along some makeup?''

Kicky gasped. ''Are your parents also friends with somebody who owns a makeup company?''

I chuckled. ''No, not exactly. But I could, you know, buy some.''

''Buy some?''

''Sure. You said yourself that everybody who comes to a make-over night is expected to bring something for the group. So how about if I bring makeup?''

''Sure!'' Kicky cried. In fact, she sounded so excited that I half expected her to come jumping through the telephone. ''That would be terrific, Samantha! Now make sure you get a variety of shades. We all have very different coloring, so we'll all need different colors of blush and eyeshadow. . . ."

"Uh, okay, Kicky—"

"And I've always wanted to try that mascara that comes in colors like blue and green and violet. I'd love it if you could get some of those."

"Sure. I'll try, but—"

"And make sure you don't get any of that cheap stuff. I hate it when makeup has too much perfume in it, don't you? Sometimes it even makes me sneeze, and I just want to *die* when my nose gets all red."

"Right. Lots of shades of blush and eyeshadow, different colors of mascara, high-quality brands. . . . I think I've got it."

"Oh, Samantha! We're all going to have such fun. I can hardly wait!"

"Me, either."

"You know what? I'm happier than ever that I decided to invite you."

As I hung up the telephone, my head was buzzing. The items on my brand-new shopping list were dancing in my head. Mascara, eyeshadow, blush . . . this make-over night was turning out to be expensive.

Don't be so petty, I told myself firmly. What does it matter if making a reasonable contribution to make-over night costs a few dollars? It's not as if I don't have the money. What *does* matter is that Kicky and her friends are trying to be friendly. They're reaching out to me, trying to get to know me a little, inviting me to join their crowd. . . .

What could possibly be wrong with that?

* * *

The next morning, I walked into first-period English class and found Betsy and Carla chattering away. Mr. Homer, our teacher, was up at the front of the room, crouched down low, muttering to himself as he picked up paper clips, one at a time. Apparently, only seconds before he had dropped an entire box of five hundred.

"Hi, Carla. Hi, Betsy!" I said brightly, plopping down into my seat.

"Oh, good," Carla breathed. "Samantha's here."

"Now *that's* a nice greeting," I returned, smiling.

"What Carla means," Betsy said, "is that we've been waiting for you. We need you to be the tie breaker in the little discussion the two of us have been having."

I nodded, then said seriously, "That sounds like quite a responsibility, especially at eight twenty-five in the morning. But I can handle it."

"Okay. Betsy and I have been trying to decide what the three of us should do tomorrow night. She wants to go to the movies, over at the mall. But *I* say the theaters are always packed on Friday night. I'd much rather we all went to my house to watch a video."

"I love videos," Betsy said, "but there's nothing that can match the excitement of seeing a film in a real live movie theater. Besides, I always find that going to the movies is a terrific way of celebrating the end of a long, hard week."

"So, Sam, there it is. Friday night at the movies versus Friday night watching a rented video." Carla shrugged. "You're the tie breaker. What's it going to be?"

I gulped. "Tomorrow night?"

"Yes, Sam, tomorrow night." Teasingly, Betsy added, "Or did somebody decide that, this week, we'd skip right from Thursday to Saturday?"

I found myself wishing that were the case.

"Uh, to tell you the truth, I, uh, have other plans for tomorrow night."

Carla looked surprised—and hurt. "Other plans? But Sam! The Bubble Gum Gang *always* spends Friday nights together."

"I know. But this week, something special came up."

"What is it?" Betsy asked. The look on her face was sympathetic. "Some family thing you can't get out of?"

"Not exactly." I glanced over at Mr. Homer. I wished he would hurry up with his silly paper clips so he could call the class to order. After all, the bell had already rung. But he was barely halfway through. There were still tiny bits of metal strewn everywhere. "You see, this really funny thing happened last night when I came home from baby-sitting."

All of a sudden Betsy slapped her hand against her forehead. "Of course! Baby-sitting! I forgot all about the fact that last night was your first time baby-sitting. How did it go, Sam? Wasn't it a breeze?"

"I wouldn't say it was a *breeze*, exactly. . . ."

"I want to hear all about it," Carla said. "But let's get this settled first, okay?"

"Maybe Sam has to baby-sit for the McArdles again," Betsy said. "Is that it, Samantha?"

I looked at Mr. Homer again. He seemed to be

dropping more paper clips than he was managing to pick up. I decided just to dive right in.

"I'm going over to Kicky's house tomorrow night."

"What?" Carla gasped.

Betsy, meanwhile, was laughing. "Okay, Sam. Very funny. Now tell us the truth, okay? What are you *really* doing tomorrow night?"

"I really am going to Kicky's house," I repeated. "She called me last night and invited me, and I said yes."

All traces of laughter faded from Betsy's face. "You're not kidding, are you?"

"Well . . . no." I was squirming back and forth in my seat.

"You're serious?" Carla said slowly. "You really are going over to Kicky's house? Sam, what on earth for?"

"She and a bunch of her friends are having a make-over night, and, well, they invited me."

"A *make-over* night?" Betsy repeated.

At that point I was thinking of going up to the front of the room and scooping up the rest of Mr. Homer's runaway paper clips myself.

"Is Wendy Lipton going to be there, too?" Carla demanded. "You know, she and I were rivals for the same part in the school play. And now you're starting to hang out with her? My goodness, Sam. Where's your sense of loyalty?"

"It's just this once," I said in a small voice. I was keeping my eyes glued to the edge of my desk. I had never noticed before that there was a tiny crack along one side.

"But why would you want to go over to Kicky's house—even once?" Betsy asked. I could tell she was truly mystified.

"Well . . . mainly because she asked me. I mean, if somebody makes a friendly gesture toward you, you'd have to be a real creep to laugh in her face."

"But *Kicky*?" Carla was saying. "Kicky Blake . . . and Wendy Lipton?"

"Jennifer Wills and Bobbi Carter will be there, too," I said quickly. "Anyway, it's just a chance to do something a little different, that's all. And to tell you the truth, I'm kind of flattered that they invited me. It's not every day that the most popular girls at school decide to include me in one of their get-togethers."

Betsy looked at me with narrowed eyes. "Samantha, this doesn't have anything to do with those hair ornaments, does it?"

"What are you talking about?" I blinked a few times, trying to look innocent.

"*Now* I get it," said Carla. "You show up in school giving out hair ornaments like Santa Claus, and the next thing you know Wendy and Kicky want to be your best friend."

"That's not it at all!" I insisted. "You're not being fair to Kicky and Wendy!"

"Believe me, Sam, I *know* those two," Carla said. "And I wouldn't trust them as far as I could throw."

"Don't you think other people could like me for myself?" I asked indignantly. I had raised my head about six inches higher.

Betsy and Carla looked at each other.

"Not Wendy and Kicky," Carla concluded.

"Look, Sam, they're the kind of girls who use people," Betsy said in a pleading voice. "Of course there are people who like you for yourself. You're looking at two very good examples. But you know as well as I do that a girl like Kicky does not suddenly show an interest in becoming somebody's friend without there being a good reason."

I opened my mouth to defend myself—*and* Kicky and Wendy, too—once again. But before I could get another word out, Mr. Homer stood up in the middle of the silver pool of paper clips.

"Okay, class. I'm going to have to leave these for later. Just make sure you don't slip on them if you walk by. Now, let's open our English grammar books to page fifty-six so we can learn more about the exciting semicolon. . . ."

Never before in my life had I been so glad to be studying punctuation. I just shrugged, giving Betsy and Carla a look that was half-apologetic and half-pleading. Then I turned away, already leafing through my grammar book, looking for page fifty-six.

I knew that my two best friends only wanted the best for me, and that they were trying to protect me. And deep down, I suspected that there was at least some truth in what they were saying. But at the moment, I didn't want to think about any of that. All I wanted to think about was that, for once in my life, the coolest crowd at school wanted to include *me*, Samantha Langtree.

* * *

"Even if you're busy Friday night, you can still come over to my house now," Betsy said to me right after school. The last bell had rung only minutes before, and the two of us were filing out of the building. "Carla has a play rehearsal today, but that doesn't mean you and I can't get together."

Ordinarily, I would have jumped at the chance to go over to Betsy's. Today, however, things were not quite so simple.

"Gee, thanks, Betsy. But, uh, I have an errand to do."

"That's okay," she said cheerfully. "I'll just come along. This happens to be one of those days when I don't have very much homework. I'm free as a bird!"

The errand, of course, was shopping for makeup for Kicky's make-over night. I had planned to head for the mall right after school. In fact, there was a wad of bills stuffed into my purse exactly for that purpose.

Now, suddenly, I found myself feeling guilty about my errand. So guilty, in fact, that I wanted to make sure Betsy didn't find out about it.

"Thanks, but, uh, this is something I have to do by myself."

Betsy stopped in her tracks. She turned to look at me. The look on her face was one of deep concern.

"Samantha, is everything all right?"

I gulped. "Of course everything is all right. Why shouldn't it be?"

"I don't know." She shook her head, as if she were confused. "All I do know is that something just doesn't *feel* right. You're acting so funny."

"I'm not acting funny!" I protested. "Just because I don't want to tell you every single detail about my life doesn't mean I'm acting funny."

She looked startled. "Of course you don't have to tell me everything, Sam. It's just . . . Oh, I don't know."

She shrugged, then looked away. We started walking again. She was still looking away as she said in a casual voice, "This doesn't happen to have anything to do with Kicky Blake, does it?"

Suddenly I was irritated at being put on the spot. Why on earth was Betsy questioning me like this?

"As a matter of fact, it does," I said coolly. "It just so happens that I'm going to the mall to pick up a few things for the make-over party Friday night."

"A few things?" she repeated. "Like what?"

"Like some makeup, that's all. The way these parties of hers work is that everybody contributes something. And my contribution just happens to be makeup."

Betsy peered at me. "What do you mean, everybody contributes something? What are the other girls contributing?"

"Oh, I don't know. Somebody rents a video. Somebody else supplies the snacks. It's really no big deal, Betsy."

But she wasn't ready to let it go. "Wait a minute. It only costs a couple of dollars to rent a video. And a bag of pretzels doesn't cost much more than that. But *makeup* . . . ?"

"Listen, what difference does it make?" I challenged. By now, my irritation was showing. Even more than that: it was taking over. "The way I spend my money is my business, Betsy Crane. And the way I spend my Friday evenings is my business, too!"

The look on Betsy's face immediately made me regret what I had just said—not to mention the way I had said it. "Gosh, Betsy, I'm sorry," I quickly told her. "I didn't mean that the way it came out. . . ."

"You're absolutely right, Samantha," she said coldly. "The way you spend your money and your time *is* your business. Far be it from me—just because I'm one of your very best friends and all—to get involved in telling you how to run your life."

"Listen, Betsy, I didn't mean—"

"But let me just say one thing. That is, *if* you don't mind spending some of your valuable time listening to me. Sooner or later, you're going to realize what Kicky and Wendy and her cute little crowd are all about. And you're also going to realize who your true friends are. I just hope that you don't get too hurt between now and the time you finally check into reality."

She stalked off, leaving me standing all alone in the schoolyard.

chapter
six

While I thought I had been nervous about my first baby-sitting job two nights earlier, that turned out to be nothing compared to how I felt on Friday night. There was an entire flock of butterflies fluttering around in my stomach as I stood on Kicky Blake's doorstep at seven o'clock sharp. I was hanging on to my bag of brand-new makeup for dear life. Meanwhile, I was dressed in what I hoped was a cool outfit.

Choosing what to wear had turned out to be a lot harder than I ever would have expected. Since I buy a lot of my clothes when my family is traveling, shopping in stores and boutiques anywhere from New York to Paris to London, they don't always look exactly like the clothes the other girls at my school wear. The colors and styles that are popular in Paris, for example, are always at least two years ahead of what the stores are selling here, even in cities like New York where they pride themselves on being a step ahead.

Usually, that doesn't faze me at all. In fact, I like wearing clothes that nobody else has—especially when I know that the outfit I'm wearing is the style featured in the pages of the top French fashion magazines, magazines like *Elle* and *French Vogue*. On this particular Friday night, however, I wanted desperately to look like everybody else. Or if not everybody else, then at least Kicky and Wendy and their crowd.

You see, I wanted them to like me.

That, as they say, is a real understatement. The truth was, I felt like I was going for a job interview. Or maybe the way Carla felt when she went up on stage and auditioned for a part in the school production of *Our Town*. At any rate, I was frantic. I wanted desperately to be accepted. And looking the part, I decided, would go a long way toward making that happen. I ended up wearing an outfit I had gotten in Paris two years earlier, a stretchy pair of pants and an oversized shirt in outrageous colors that was pretty much in line with what the cheerleaders of Hanover Junior High were into.

Still, knowing I probably looked okay wasn't enough to make all those butterflies go away. As I rang Kicky's doorbell, my mouth was dry, and my knees were shaking.

It occurred to me that this would be an excellent time to go jogging.

But before I had a chance to act on it, Kicky was at the door, all smiles. She was wearing almost the exact same thing I was wearing. I let out a loud sigh of relief.

"Samantha! You made it!"

"Just barely," I returned.

"You look terrific. I *love* that outfit."

"Thanks." I gulped. Something came over me—some strange, sudden burst of confidence—and I decided to take a chance. "I bought this in Paris a couple of years ago."

"Paris?" Kicky breathed. "Paris, France?"

"That's the one."

Instead of looking at me like I was weird, she actually looked impressed. "Oooh. Paris. I've never been further than Springfield. I'm so *jealous*, Samantha! Well, come on in. Wendy and Bobbi and Jen are already upstairs, stuffing their faces." She rolled her eyes upward. "I just hope we don't all get fat. After all, we wouldn't want to end up looking like—"

Suddenly she froze. "What I mean is, since this is a make-over night and all and we're all trying to find ways to make ourselves look better. . . ."

But it was too late. I knew exactly what she had planned to say.

She was going to say, "We wouldn't want to end up looking like Carla Farrell."

Kicky wasn't the only one who froze. I did kind of a snowman act myself, mainly because I didn't know what to say or do, either. Should I rush to Carla's defense? Should I turn around and walk right out of there, never to return? Or should I just pretend I didn't understand?

Before I had a chance to make a decision, Kicky grabbed my arm and started half leading, half dragging me up the stairs. By the time we were halfway up, I had already convinced myself that simply pretending I hadn't understood what she was saying was the easiest way to handle this.

Suddenly Kicky pointed to my small blue shopping bag.

"Oooh, is that the makeup?" she cried, her eyes lighting up.

I nodded. "I remembered what you said about not buying the cheap stuff, so I got Madame Romaine." Anxiously, I added, "I hope that's okay."

"Samantha, Madame Romaine cosmetics are the *best*," Kicky cooed. "To tell you the truth, whenever I buy makeup, I always get one of the drug-store brands. It's all I can afford."

I opened my mouth in surprise. But I never did get a chance to say anything. The moment we hit the top of the stairs, Kicky yelled, "She's here!" A stampede of three came running out to the hallway from one of the bedrooms.

"Samantha!" Wendy cried. "We're so glad you could come!"

"You look nice," Jennifer Carter said. "Hey, what's in the bag?"

"Um, just some makeup," I said. I was suddenly feeling shy. "It was, um, Kicky's idea."

"Oh, great." Bobbi was already peering into the bag. "I can't *wait* to try it."

"Let's spill the bag out onto the bed," Wendy suggested.

"Gee, look at this. Madame Romaine." Bobbi's voice was practically a whisper.

Jennifer was jumping up and down. "I get to choose the blush I want first!"

The four of them galloped back into the bedroom,

with Bobbi clutching my shopping bag. I, meanwhile, was left standing alone in the hall.

Suddenly Kicky turned back. "Well, come *on*, Samantha," she insisted with a smile. "We want you to be part of this, too!"

I stood in the doorway of her bedroom, feeling awkward. I just watched as the four of them dumped the shopping bag out on Kicky's bed and began pawing through the makeup.

"Wow, look at this eyeshadow!" cried Bobbi, holding up a small case with four different shades of green. "This is going to look great with my green eyes!"

"Let me see that." Wendy grabbed it out of her hand. "Oh, I love this! I want to try it, right after you. Hey, check out that red lipstick. Gosh, I've never even tried on red before."

It didn't take long for the contents of the bag to be divided up into four piles. It was as if Wendy, Kicky, Jennifer and Bobbi had completely forgotten I was there. Finally, I took a little step forward and cleared my throat.

"Uh, Wendy, since you and I have the same kind of coloring, maybe we should both try on the same makeup."

Wendy looked up, blinking. The others fell silent. For a moment all four girls just stared at me.

And then Wendy said, "Oh, sure, Samantha. That's a great idea."

"But how about if we watch the video first?" I went on boldly.

"Video?" Bobbie repeated. "What video?"

"Oh, I'm the one who told Samantha about that," Kicky said quickly. "I said that sometimes when we do these make-over nights, somebody brings along a video. You know, one of those exercise tapes, or maybe one on makeup techniques or hairstyles."

Jennifer and Wendy looked at each other. "Videos?" they said at the same time.

Bobbi started to turn pink. "Oh, that's right. Now I remember. Kicky, you told me to bring a video along tonight."

"Did you?" she asked.

"Well . . . actually, to tell you the truth, I didn't have the money." She was staring at the tube of lipstick she was clutching in her hand.

"Oh, that's okay," I said quickly. It was funny; somehow, I had ended up feeling that Bobbi not having enough money to rent a video had something to do with me.

"But maybe you'd like something to eat," Kicky said. "Here, have some popcorn." She held out a nearly empty bowl, meanwhile shrugging her shoulders. "Sorry, but that's all there was. I guess we just kind of ran out."

"That's all right. I'm not very hungry."

Bobbi turned to Kicky. "What are we waiting for? Are we going to try on this cool makeup or not?"

Without waiting another moment, the other four girls grabbed their piles of goodies and staked out spots in front of a mirror. Immediately they became absorbed in putting it on—so much, in fact, that to me they looked more like clowns than anything else.

"Oooh, don't you *love* this purple eyeshadow on me?" Kicky cried. "I look like a model!"

"This peach blush is the best," Jennifer was muttering. "It goes on so smoothly. I guess it really pays to buy the better-quality stuff."

I simply watched. Finally, Kicky noticed that I wasn't part of the giggling and oohing and ahhing that went along with the other girls' love affair with the makeup I'd brought along.

"How about you, Samantha?" she asked, glancing over at me, a wand of jade green mascara poised in midair. "Don't you want to try some of this?"

"Well, to tell you the truth, I don't really have a lot of experience with makeup."

"All the more reason to jump in. Besides," she added, putting down the mascara, "I know a little secret that would give you a good reason to want to look your best."

I had no idea what she was talking about. "What?"

Kicky giggled. "Oh, let's just say that there's a certain boy at our school who has—shall we say—expressed an interest in one Samantha Langtree."

I just stared at her. "Who?"

Still giggling, Kicky said, "Well, I don't know if I should tell you his name. I mean, the only way I even know about it is that I overheard him talking to one of his friends. But I wouldn't want word to get out that I'm somebody who goes around spying on people or anything. . . ."

"Who? Who?" Jennifer demanded.

"I bet I know," Bobbi said.

"Tell me," I pleaded. Suddenly, nothing in the

entire world seemed to matter as much as finding out which boy she had overheard talking about me—in a positive way, no less. "Please, Kicky!"

She peered at her reflection in the mirror. "You know, what I really need is some jade green eyeshadow to go with this green mascara."

"I'll get you some," I offered. "I'll go to the mall this weekend."

"You will?" Kicky looked over at me, blinking in surprise. "Why, Samantha, that's so *sweet* of you. Thank you. You're very thoughtful. No wonder Jason Downing was talking about how nice you are."

She clasped her hand over her mouth, her eyes growing wide. "Oh, my gosh. I *told*."

"Jason Downing?" I repeated. I wasn't quite sure whether or not to believe her. Jason, after all, is probably the most popular boy at school. Not only is he one of the Hanover Junior High's top football players, he also happens to have blond hair, blue eyes, and a face that looks like it belongs on a movie screen.

I found myself reporting to Kicky, "Jason Downing is in my English class."

"Well, then, I guess that's where he first noticed you," she said matter-of-factly. "You know, I've known Jason since second grade. He lives practically across the street. I'll tell you what. The next time I see him, I'll make a point of mentioning that you came over to my house tonight, and that we all think you're really terrific. I'll see if I can find out anything else, too."

I smiled weakly. "Maybe I will try some of that green mascara."

By the end of the evening, I looked as pretty and as sophisticated as a model. At least, that's what Kicky and Wendy and the others kept telling me. Actually, I felt like I was dressed up for Halloween, but I decided to keep that to myself.

"What should we do with this makeup?" Jennifer asked late that night as we were all getting ready to leave. "I guess you want it all back, Samantha, right?"

"Oh, no!" I insisted. "I bought it for all of you. It was my contribution to the make-over night."

Jennifer and Bobbi looked at each other, surprised.

"Wow," Jennifer breathed. "Thanks a lot, Samantha."

"Boy, Samantha," Bobbi said. "I sure was wrong about you. We all were, I guess."

"Excuse me?" I asked. Out of the corner of my eye, I noticed that Kicky had just grabbed Wendy's arm.

Bobbi, however, didn't notice at all. "We used to think you were a real snob, since you were so rich and all. Who would ever have thought you'd turn out to be okay?"

I supposed I should have felt complimented. At least, as I walked home, I kept telling myself that that was the way Bobbi meant what she said.

"You just made four brand-new friends," I muttered aloud. "Four girls—four really popular girls— who want you to be part of their crowd. You should be feeling terrific. Anybody would."

Which made it all that much harder to understand

why, underneath it all, what I was actually feeling was kind of uncomfortable, as if I were wearing a pair of shoes that didn't quite fit right. Or maybe the wrong shade of eyeshadow.

chapter
seven

That same feeling was still with me the next day, the feeling that, somehow, something wasn't quite right. I decided to try to shake it off, to distract myself by doing something fun. Fortunately, a golden opportunity to do exactly that fell right smack into my lap.

"Who wants to go horseback riding?" my father asked jovially over breakfast on Saturday morning.

It was one of those perfect autumn days. The air was crisp and energizing. The brilliant colors of autumn were everywhere, bright oranges and golds and reds that made it impossible to stay indoors. But it was still early, and everyone in my family was sitting around in pajamas, eating breakfast and trying to decide how to use this rare, perfect day.

My dad, I could see, had already decided. And his idea sounded wonderful to me.

"I'd love to," I exclaimed. "When do we leave?"

"Right after breakfast," he replied. "Any more takers?"

"Thanks, but I'm going over to the nature preserve

with Katherine for a long walk.'' My mother smiled at my younger sister. ''You know I try to spend time with each of my girls, one at a time. This morning, it's Katherine's turn.''

''I'm going biking with my friends,'' Elizabeth said. ''Sorry, Dad. Maybe next time.''

''I guess it's just you and me, then,'' my father said to me. Actually, he looked pleased.

''Gosh, it's beautiful out here,'' I said to my father an hour later. He and I were sitting upon two of our favorite horses from the local stable, enjoying the gorgeous colors of the changing leaves as we made our way slowly down one of the bridle paths. Later on, I knew, we would canter through the woods, urging our horses, Coffee and Smiley, to go faster and faster. But for now, we were using our time alone together just to talk.

''Yes, it is beautiful,'' my father agreed. ''Horseback riding is one of my favorite ways of relaxing after a long, difficult week. I love the animals, of course. And I find it exhilarating, being so close to nature. . . .''

He let out a long, sad sigh. ''I just hope we don't have to give it up.''

''Give it up?'' I cried. ''Daddy, what are you talking about?''

He looked over at me, a serious expression on his face. ''Samantha, there's something I want to talk to you about. I was actually glad that your mother and sisters didn't want to come along today. I wanted the chance to talk to you alone. I don't mean to burden you, but you are a good listener. Besides, I feel you really understand.''

"What is it, Daddy?" This time my voice was much more gentle.

He sighed again. "Sam, I'm afraid that my company is having some real problems. Financial problems.''

I nodded. "You mentioned that last week, the night Ellsworth von Thornbottom and his family came over for dinner.''

"It's the same old problem. Langtree Industries' competitors keep beating us in the race to develop new products.'' He shook his head slowly. "If this trend continues, Samantha, our family is going to have to cut back. The little extras, like horseback riding on Saturday mornings, are going to have to go.''

"That's all right, Daddy," I was quick to reassure him. "Katherine and Elizabeth and I would understand. We could all tighten our belts. We wouldn't mind a bit. Honest!''

"Thank you, Samantha.'' My father looked over at me and smiled sadly. "Thank you for being so understanding. And for being so supportive.''

"Besides,'' I told him, "now that I'm working, I won't need to come to you for spending money as often.''

"I'm really glad that's going so well. As a matter of fact, Steve McArdle mentioned to me that you were one of the best baby-sitters he and his wife have ever had.''

I gave him a weak smile. When my father had eagerly asked me how my first evening at the McArdles' had gone, all I had said was that it had been fine. My stomach gave a little lurch as I remembered that tonight, I would be going back for more.

I was afraid he would start asking me more about it. Instead, my father didn't seem to be paying very close attention. He was lost in thought.

"You know, Sam," he finally said, "there is one hope for my company."

"What's that?"

"We've been developing an exciting new product. I haven't said a word to anybody—not even to your mother—because it's so hush-hush. But we're planning to come out with it next month, so I think I can tell my favorite horseback riding partner about it."

I smiled, proud to be let in on a top-level secret.

"Langtree Industries has been developing a new type of computer that could well revolutionize education in this country. It's a computer specially designed to help children learn, one that's actually more like a robot than a simple computer. For one thing, it's voice activated."

"Voice activated?" I repeated. "What does that mean?"

"It means that you talk to the computer the same way you would talk to a person, using your voice to communicate instead of pushing buttons on a keyboard. You don't type in the words, 'I don't know the answer'; you simply *tell* it, and it responds. It can understand the human voice. We call it VAC-Man— *V* for voice, *A* for activated, *C* for computer."

"That *is* exciting, Daddy!"

"The idea of voice-activated computers isn't brand

new. It's the way we're using it for educational programs that's so original. Sam, I have a feeling that when we come out with VAC-Man, Langtree Industries is going to become the number-one computer company in the country!"

"Oh, Daddy, I knew you'd do it! I knew you'd find a way to fix your company's financial problems."

For the first time since we'd started talking, my father actually looked hopeful.

"But enough about the business!" he suddenly cried. "Let's get these horses moving, Sam. Race you to the lake!"

There I was again, standing outside the McArdles' house. Once again, I was armed with art supplies, games, puzzles, and the children's books I'd taken out of the library. What I should have brought, I was thinking, was a mop, a bucket, and a bottle of all-purpose cleaner.

"She's here! She's here!" As soon as I walked in the front door, the three McArdle Monsters came scrambling down the stairs. Patty was first, her long brown hair flying wildly behind her. Jimmy was right behind her, holding little Willy around the stomach and lugging him around as if he were a very heavy teddy bear.

"Are you going to read bedtime stories to us tonight?" Patty instantly demanded. "I've been waiting to hear that one about the bunnies."

"And I want you to read me *The Little Engine That Could*," Jimmy said. "You are going to read to us, right?"

"It depends," I replied calmly. "Patty, Jimmy, are *you* going to behave tonight?"

Both of them nodded.

"My goodness," Mr. McArdle said, "I must say, Samantha, I am very impressed. It looks as if you already have this situation well under control."

"Well, Mr. McArdle, I've found that—"

"We'd better get going, dear," interrupted his wife. "The Stones said seven-fifteen on the dot, and you know how prompt they always are."

"Could you please write down the Stones' telephone number for me?" I reminded them.

Mr. McArdle gestured in the direction of the den. "Oh, it's written down in our address book. I'm sure you'll be able to find it. That is, if you really need it." He gave me a meaningful look, then was out the door.

"Well, now," I said, turning to my three charges. "What would you like to do tonight? I brought puzzles, games, some markers in neon colors. . . ."

"I want to show you the new dollhouse my daddy just bought me," Patty announced proudly. "Come upstairs to my room."

With little Willy nestled comfortably in my arms, I followed her up the stairs. Jimmy was right behind me. "A new dollhouse?" I said, trying to be polite. "Is it your birthday, Patty?"

She gave me an odd look. "Of course not. Why, what difference would that make?"

As I went into Patty's room, I was expecting to see something simple, perhaps a little cardboard house set up on the dresser. I certainly was surprised, for what I found was sitting in the middle of the rug, practically filling the entire room.

"Patty!" I gasped. "This is unbelievable!"

I had seen this kind of dollhouse before—in toy museums. It was made of wood, modeled after those old-fashioned Victorian houses with turrets and towers and wonderful gingerbread trim. It was four stories high, standing almost as tall as I was. There was a living room, dining room, and kitchen on the first floor, three bedrooms on the second floor, a sewing room and a playroom on the third, and an attic with a sloping ceiling on top.

Every room was decorated as carefully as if it were a real house. There was wallpaper on the walls and tiny rugs on the floors. There was little furniture, too, the really well made kind. Every other detail had been taken care of as well. There were itsy-bitsy plates of pretend food on the kitchen table, small hatboxes in the closets, even an eensy-beensy mouse eating a speck of yellow cheese in the attic.

"Patty, this is amazing!" I breathed. And it must have cost a small fortune, I was thinking. What an elaborate present for a little girl . . . and it's not even her birthday.

"That's nothing," Jimmy said. "You should see the ten-speed bike my dad got me."

A ten-speed bike . . . for a seven-year-old, a little boy who had probably just mastered the art of riding a bicycle without training wheels?

"It's out in the garage," Jimmy went on. "Come on out and see it. I'll even let you try it, if you want."

"A new bike . . . a new dollhouse . . ." I gulped.

"Are you *sure* none of this is for some special occasion?"

Patty and Jimmy looked at each other and shrugged.

"What's the big deal?" Jimmy asked.

"Your father didn't get a raise or a promotion at work or anything like that?" I asked.

Patty shook her head. "Daddy is always buying us neat presents."

"I'll tell you what, Patty," I told her. "After Jimmy shows me his new bike, we can come back here and play with your dollhouse."

I expected her face to light up. Or at least for her to say something like, "Oh, boy!" Instead, she turned to me and said, "Gee, Sam, I was hoping you'd play a game with us."

"You mean you don't even want to play with your dollhouse?"

She looked at me with big, sad eyes. "I'd rather play with you."

"Okay," I assured her. "As soon as I see Jimmy's bike, we'll play a game together. All four of us." Willy clapped his hands happily, even though I suspected he had no idea what we were talking about.

In the garage, Jimmy showed me his bike. "See? Ten speeds, just like I told you. Out of all my friends, I'm the only one who has a bike like this."

"Gee, ten speeds," I said. "Do you know how to ride it yet?"

"Well . . . no."

"I bet you can't wait to learn, then."

Jimmy shrugged.

"Maybe sometime this weekend your dad will teach you how to ride it," I said.

Jimmy looked at me as if I had just told him his nose was turning green. "My dad?" he repeated.

"Yes, Jimmy, your dad."

"My dad never plays with me," he said matter-of-factly. "I already told you. He always works on the weekends."

"He works all the time," Patty said. She, too, sounded as if this were something she took for granted. "Can we play that game now?"

For the rest of the evening, Patty and Jimmy acted like angels. Well, almost. There was the argument about who really won Chutes and Ladders, and then Patty spilled her chocolate milk all over Jimmy and he started to pull her hair. Willy had a few temper tantrums of his own before he finally went to sleep in his crib, after I had sung "The Star Spangled Banner" softly, seven times in a row. But all in all, the evening went about ten thousand times better than the first night I had baby-sat.

Finally it was time for Patty and Jimmy to go to bed.

"Did we behave okay?" Patty asked anxiously. "Are you going to read to us this time?"

Both Patty and Jimmy had eaten their dinner, taken their baths, and brushed their teeth. Neither of them looked the least bit tired, but Patty was in her bed and Jimmy was at the foot, each of them clutching two of the library books they had picked out for me to read.

"Yes, I'm going to read to you," I replied. "And both of you were great, the entire evening."

I leaned over to give Patty a little kiss on the head. I couldn't resist, since she looked so sweet, sitting there with her dinosaur pajamas on, pleading with me to read her a book about bunnies. And then a surprising thing happened. She threw her arms around me, gave me a big bear hug, and said, "I love you, Sam. You're the best baby-sitter anybody ever had."

I was a little bit hoarse after I read four whole books out loud. First the bunny book for Patty, then *The Little Engine That Could*, then one more for Patty, and finally, one last one for Jimmy. But I didn't mind my sore throat at all. The two of them snuggled up against me, looking at the pictures in the books and asking questions and talking about the characters.

I could tell they were really enjoying themselves. Even more than that, I felt that in spending time with them like this, I was really giving them something special. And I was. I was giving them myself.

"Good night, Patty. Good night, Jimmy," I whispered once they were both in their own beds, fast asleep. I checked on Willy, who was in his crib, snoring away happily.

They really were pretty cute, I had to admit. I was discovering that the McArdle Monsters weren't such monsters, after all. They just needed what everybody else in the world needs. Someone to pay attention to them. Somebody to care about them. And most of all, somebody to love them.

chapter
eight

Monday morning, I was dreading going to school. The very first thing, I knew, I was going to have to confront Betsy and Carla. There was still tension in the air between me and Betsy, leftover from our talk the week before. As if that weren't bad enough, they were both sure to be full of questions about how the Friday night make-over party with Kicky and Company had gone.

That weekend had been a busy one for all of us, Carla with the school play, Betsy with a special project she was working on for school, and so I had gotten off the hook—at least for a little while. But as I went downstairs to breakfast, all I could think about were the expressions bound to be on their faces as they casually asked me for a report on life within the cheerleaders' inner circle.

"Good morning, Sam," my father greeted me as I came to the table. He glanced up from the business section of the newspaper he was reading and smiled. "All set for another week of school?"

"I guess so," I said, sitting down and reaching for

the box of corn flakes. "How about you? All set for another week of work?"

"I'd better be, especially since it's going to be a busy one." He turned back to his paper. "I just want to check on some of these stock prices. . . ."

I wasn't really paying attention as he turned the page of the newspaper. I was busy pouring corn flakes into a bowl, still thinking about Betsy and Carla and how I was going to answer all those questions they had been saving up all weekend.

And then, all of a sudden, my father yelled, "What on *earth*?"

I looked up quickly, expecting to see that he had spilled his coffee or found a stain on his necktie. But the expression on his face told me something a lot worse than that had just happened.

"What is it?" I demanded. "Daddy, you look as if you just saw a ghost!"

He didn't even look at me. He was too busy staring at the newspaper.

"Daddy? Are you okay?" By now I was getting worried. He really did look as if he'd seen a ghost, but I knew there weren't any of those in the business section of the morning newspaper.

"I can't believe it," he muttered. "I simply cannot believe it."

"*What*, Daddy?" I cried. I jumped up and ran around the table to where he was sitting, anxious to see for myself what this was all about.

Instantly, I knew. What my father was staring at was a full-page advertisement in the newspaper—an advertisement for a voice-activated computer that, ac-

cording to the ad's headline, was guaranteed to revolutionize education in this country.

"Oh, no!" I gasped. "Daddy, it's your computer!
It's VAC-Man!" I looked at the ad more closely. "But
this isn't your company's name. This says Computer
Masters. Who—or what—is Computer Masters?"

"Langtree Industries' biggest competitor, that's
who," he replied. "And it just so happens their corporate offices are located less than two miles away
from here." He closed the newspaper and pushed it
aside. "Samantha," he said earnestly, "this can only
mean one thing."

"What, Daddy?"

He looked at me with the saddest, most troubled
eyes I have ever seen.

"Somebody who works at Langtree Industries must
be selling company secrets."

As I rushed to my first-period English class, I was
no longer dreading seeing Betsy and Carla. In fact, I
could hardly wait. We Langtrees had a crisis on our
hands—and I intended to ask the Bubble Gum Gang
to pull together and help us get to the bottom of it.

I practically fell over my own feet as I came scrambling into Mr. Homer's classroom. One glance toward the front of the room told me that, as usual,
class would be starting late. At the moment, Mr.
Homer was busy lecturing a small group of students
gathered around his desk on the evils of using a semicolon where a colon belonged.

"Betsy! Carla! Boy, am I glad to see you!" I
plopped down into my chair. Given Kicky's insistence

that Jason Downing was interested in me, I had been worried that during English class I would keep sneaking glances at him in an attempt to read his mind. As it turned out, I was so upset about what had happened that morning at breakfast that I forgot all about him.

Carla and Betsy looked over at me. They both had really neutral expressions on their faces, these sort of funny half smiles that I had never seen before.

"Well, hello, Samantha," Betsy said. "How was your weekend?"

"My weekend was fine," I said impatiently. "But you've got to listen to me. Something really incredible has happened—"

"Did you have a good time at Kicky's house Friday night?" Carla interrupted.

"Yes, it was okay, I guess. But that's really not what I—"

"I'm glad you had fun, Sam," Betsy went on. "Carla and I were just saying that we wondered whether or not you had had fun at Kicky's house."

"Listen, you two!" I exploded. "Forget Kicky! Forget Friday night! Disaster has struck in the Langtree household!"

Wouldn't you know that Mr. Homer would choose that exact moment to abandon the semicolon and call the class to order?

"All right, class," he boomed. "Today we're going to delve into the exciting and often mysterious world of the apostrophe."

To make a long story short, it wasn't until after school that I finally had a chance to sit down with the other members of the Bubble Gum Gang and tell them about my father's suspicion that somebody inside Langtree Industries was selling company secrets. When I did, I thought their eyes were going to pop out of their heads.

"A corporate *spy*?" Carla gasped after I told them both the whole story.

"One of your dad's employees . . . betraying the company?" Betsy breathed.

The three of us had gathered at Betsy's house. We were sitting on the floor of her bedroom, crunching apples, our after-school snack.

"Your father must be terribly upset," Betsy continued. "What does he plan to do about it?"

"I don't know what *he* plans to do about it," I replied, "but I know what *I* plan to do about it."

"What?" Carla and Betsy asked in unison.

"Enlist the aid of the Bubble Gum Gang, that's what!" I looked hopefully from Carla to Betsy and back to Carla. "You will help me, won't you?"

"Of course we will!" Carla cried without a moment's hesitation.

"I'm just sorry we didn't think of it ourselves!" Betsy added. "After all, investigating mysteries is the Bubble Gum Gang's specialty!"

Carla nodded. "Do you have any ideas about where we should begin?"

I leaned forward, excited—and more than a little relieved—over their enthusiasm. Now that they had agreed to help, I wondered how I could ever have doubted that they would. I took a deep breath, using the time to step back and appreciate what good friends

I had in Carla and Betsy. And then I jumped right into the matter at hand.

"Actually, I do. What we need to do is get inside the offices of my father's company."

"Inside?" Carla asked doubtfully.

"Sure. I think we really need to get a close look at what goes on there. We need to see who's who, look around, keep our eyes open. . . ."

"Right," Betsy said. "Peek into a few file cabinets, listen in on a few conversations . . ."

I looked over at her and laughed. "Betsy Crane," I said, "I like the way you think."

"It sounds great," Carla said, "but how do you propose we do all that? How can we even get inside Langtree Industries in the first place?"

"I have an idea," I said softly.

Betsy didn't seem to have heard me. "I know. We could pretend we work for a temporary employment agency, and that there's been some sort of mix-up and they sent us to the wrong company. . . ."

"Or maybe we could—" I tried.

Carla was already shaking her head. "We look too young to pass for employees of one of those temp agencies. Even if we got all dressed up and put on lots of makeup, we'd still never look old enough. But I have an idea. Maybe we could pretend we're selling something . . . something to raise money for our school. You know, candy or flower seeds, something like that. Anyway, that way we could still look like junior high school students, but we'd have an excuse to be inside an office building."

"Or maybe we could try my idea—" I interjected.

"The problem with that," Betsy said in response to Carla's suggestion, "is that we wouldn't be able to stay in the office building very long. Once we had given our sales pitch, we'd have no more reason to hang around, poking around inside file cabinets and looking for employees doing suspicious things."

"Is it my turn yet?" I suddenly cried in a loud voice.

Carla and Betsy both looked over at me, blinking in surprise.

"I'm sorry, Sam," Betsy said. "Is there something you wanted to say?"

"I guess we got kind of carried away," Carla apologized. "I was really getting into brainstorming for a minute there. What's your idea, Samantha?"

"My idea," I said calmly, "is that we tell my father that we've all been assigned a new school project. One designed to help us find out what our parents really do. I'll pretend we're supposed to get together in teams of three and spend an afternoon at a parent's office, seeing firsthand what that parent's job is really all about."

I sat back, leaning against the edge of Betsy's bed, waiting to hear their reaction.

"Pure genius!" Carla cried. "I love it!"

"That really is inspired," Betsy added admiringly. "Tell me, Sam, how on earth did you ever come up with such a clever solution to our problem?"

"Easy," I replied, giggling. "Pretending we were working on a school project was *your* idea, Betsy, when we needed a way to investigate the mysterious goings-on at the mall a few weeks ago!"

Betsy laughed. "Well, Sam, you know what they say: Imitation is the sincerest form of flattery. And I feel very flattered!"

We put our heads together and started working out the details of the plan. We all agreed that the following Friday afternoon was the best time to go to my father's office. That way, we would get on the case in fairly short order, but we would at least have a few days to get ready. Another reason was that we wouldn't have to worry about getting homework done for the next day. We also had no commitments to any after-school clubs or meetings on Friday. Even the play Carla was in had no rehearsal that day. It was perfect.

"Friday is going to be a very important day," Carla observed once we had outlined our basic plan of action. "And going undercover at Langtree Industries is only part of it."

"What do you mean?" Betsy asked.

"Remember I told you that my parents promised me a frozen yogurt party when I lost five pounds? Well, as of this morning, I've lost four. I'd say there's a fairly good chance that by Friday, that fifth pound will be nothing more than a distant memory."

"Carla, that's great!" Betsy squealed.

"I'll say," I added. "Congratulations, Carla."

"Well . . . it's not definite, of course. And my parents keep telling me not to start planning the celebration until the scale hits that five pound loss mark."

"Don't worry," Betsy said. "Even if it doesn't turn out to be this Friday, it'll still be soon."

"I'm keeping my fingers crossed," Carla said. "I'm

also keeping my running shoes on, to remind me to keep exercising!''

Suddenly she grew serious. ''But that's not the most important thing we have to think about right now. Our next sleuthing assignment is only four days away! Sam, could you draw a map of your dad's office so we can start getting a feel for where everything is— you know, where the files are, where each person sits, details like that?''

I felt like hugging them both. Instead, I took a pen and paper out of my purse. ''Okay. The entrance is down here. . . .''

If anybody was going to get to the bottom of this, I was convinced, it would be the dedicated members of the Bubble Gum Gang.

Over dinner, I mentioned the ''school project'' to my dad—and he was more than happy to give my friends and me permission to spend a few hours after school nosing around his office. Right after dessert, I put a call in to Carla to tell her the good news. Betsy was next on the list. Needless to say, they were both thrilled.

By that point, I was so full of our plans for our undercover investigation of the dirty doings at Langtree Industries that I had all but forgotten about Kicky Blake and her crowd. So I was caught a little bit off guard when, later on that evening, the telephone rang and I picked it up to hear Kicky's chirpy voice say, ''Hello, Samantha!''

''Kicky!'' I replied. ''Uh, how are you?''

''Oh, I'm fine. And I must say,'' she added with a

giggle, "I've never *looked* better, either. Between the hair stuff you gave me last week and that wonderful makeup you brought over on Friday night, I look at least fifteen!"

"That's great." Actually, I was barely listening. Instead, I was thinking about how the Bubble Gum Gang could find out as much as possible in as short a time as possible, once we were inside my father's offices.

Maybe Kicky picked up on my lack of interest. "But that's not why I'm calling," she said quickly. "I just heard something really exciting, and I couldn't wait to tell you!"

"What is it, Kicky?" I asked.

She answered in this annoying singsong voice. "It's about Jason Downing."

Still, she had gotten my attention. I found myself remembering that there was life outside of Langtree Industries. "Jason Downing?" I repeated, my voice nearly a whisper.

"Oh, Samantha, you simply *have* to hang out with me and Wendy and everybody this weekend!" Kicky cooed. "I overheard Jason talking to one of his friends this afternoon. This Friday, Jason is going to the movies over at the mall!"

Friday evening. That rang a bell—sort of. But in my surprise over hearing from Kicky, my mind had gone blank. "So?"

"So? *So*?" Kicky giggled. "Goodness, Samantha, you'd think you'd never made a play for a boy before! What that *means*, silly, is that *you* should go to the movies at the mall, too!"

"Oh. I get it."

"Sure. If you want Jason to notice you—and to think you hang out with the right crowd and all—it's important that you start being seen with us. Especially in places where we know Jason is going to be."

"Okay." That seemed to make sense, in a strange sort of way.

"And the movie he's seeing is supposed to be really good. It's that new spy thriller that everybody's talking about."

"Oh, yes. I wanted to see that one."

"Well, Samantha, here's your golden opportunity!" Kicky giggled again. But then, suddenly, she grew quiet. "There's only one small problem."

"What's that, Kicky?"

"Well . . . you see, Wendy and Jennifer and Bobbi and I all really want to go to the movie with you. You know, to lend you moral support, and to show Jason how much we like you and everything."

"So what's the problem?"

Kicky cleared her throat. "It's not a *problem*, really. . . . It's just that, right now, some of us are a little short of funds." She went on, talking really fast. "But we were thinking that it would be a real shame for us—I mean, for *you*—to miss out on an incredible opportunity like this just because the rest of us don't have the cash right now. It's not as if we don't intend to pay you back or anything. But if you could just lend us the money for the movie . . . Honestly, Samantha, I wouldn't be asking you this if I didn't believe deep down in my heart that this was the chance of a lifetime."

"Friday night, huh? This Friday?" My mind was racing. Suddenly I remembered. The yogurt party! Still, that wasn't definite . . . and this *was* the chance of a lifetime, just as Kicky had said. Still, I kept thinking about how excited Carla had looked when she told me about those four pounds she had lost. . . .

"You know, Samantha, you are *so* lucky," Kicky said with a sigh. "I was watching Jason today in math class, and he is simply the cutest boy who ever walked the halls of Hanover Junior High School. Did you ever notice how blue his eyes are? If he was ever interested in me, I think I would just roll over and die. Oooh, I wish I were you!"

I swallowed hard. And then, closing my eyes to try to shut out the image of Carla beaming at me, I said, "Friday night sounds great, Kicky."

"Goody!" Kicky squealed. "I'm telling you, Samantha, you won't regret this. Oooh, we're all going to have so much fun!"

I had opened my eyes by then. It was just as well, since I had found that even with them closed, I still couldn't get Carla's face out of my mind.

chapter
nine

The next few days whizzed by so quickly that I forgot all about Carla and the possibility of her party at Yo-Yo's Yogurt. Between keeping up with my schoolwork and plotting the Bubble Gum Gang's undercover operation at Langtree Industries, my mind was so full that my social life quickly took a backseat.

Finally, Friday afternoon rolled around. I was filled with a mixture of dread and excited anticipation as I closed the metal door of my locker. I was also nervous, I realized when I nearly jumped out of my skin at the slamming sound echoing through the nearly empty hallways of Hanover Junior High. But there was little time for thinking about those butterflies that were making a return visit to my stomach. Betsy and Carla and I had agreed to meet outside the front entrance of the school at three o'clock sharp.

Just as I expected, they were right on time.

"Samantha!" Betsy cried, sounding panicked. "As I was running over here, I realized that we forgot one important detail!"

"What?" My heart was jumping up and down as if it were doing aerobic exercises.

"How are we going to get to your father's office?"

"Oh, is *that* all." My heart flopped back down where it belonged. "Don't worry. That's all been taken care of."

"How are we going to get there?" asked Carla. "Are we taking a bus? Or maybe a taxi?"

I didn't have a chance to answer. Just then, a long, sleek, black limousine turned the corner and pulled up in front of the school.

"You're kidding," Betsy breathed.

I glanced over at Carla. Her eyes were as round as the shiny hubcaps on the car.

"It's the company car," I said with a shrug. "Actually, it was Dad's idea. Come on, I'll race you."

Even after the three of us had settled into the backseat of the limo, and its driver, Thomas, was gliding out of the school parking lot, Carla's eyes were still wide with astonishment.

"Honestly, Samantha," she finally said, "I had no idea we were going in such style!"

"Wait until you see this." I started opening the various compartments hidden beneath the powder blue velour fabric that covered the seats, the floors, even the ceiling of the car. "Here's a car phone. This is a CD player. Oh, and here's the refrigerator. Would anybody like something cold to drink?"

Betsy was laughing. "Nothing like making a grand entrance!"

Suddenly she grew serious. "But don't you think the Bubble Gum Gang should be more secretive? After all, we are planning to do a little bit more than simply learn about what makes a computer company tick.''

I shook my head. ''I *want* everybody to know we're there. That way, we'll have no problem getting permission to check out every nook and cranny, peek into every file cabinet, and examine every square inch of Langtree Industries until we come up with something that looks suspicious.''

Betsy stroked the soft blue fabric covering the seat. ''Even if we don't find out a thing, Sam, this is still going to be a day I will never forget.''

''Speaking of forgetting . . .'' Carla suddenly cried, ''I've been so busy thinking about today's adventure that I almost forgot to tell you my big news!''

My heart sank. Even as Betsy was saying, ''What's that, Carla?'' I knew what she was going to say. The party at Yo-Yo's. I would have bet my father's company limousine that that was what she was talking about.

I would have won the bet.

''I lost five pounds!'' Carla examined. ''I stepped on the scale this morning and there it was!''

''Congratulations!'' Betsy leaned over and hugged her. ''Carla, that is so great. I'm thrilled for you.''

''My parents were thrilled, too,'' Carla said proudly. ''So thrilled, in fact, that they told me to go ahead and invite the two of you to an all-you-can-eat frozen yogurt party at Yo-Yo's. It's tonight around seven.''

''I'll be there!'' Betsy assured her. ''Yum. I can practically taste the vanilla topped with fresh strawberries already!'' She glanced over at me. ''How about you, Sam? You're coming, aren't you?''

Fortunately, the limousine had just pulled up in front of my father's office building.

''We're here,'' I announced with a gulp.

The catch in my voice was only partly due to my nervousness about the undercover expedition we were about to begin. Carla's celebration really was going on tonight—at the exact same time that I was supposed to be going to the movies with Kicky and her friends. Sure, I had known all along it was a possibility. I had just been unwilling to think about it.

I was certainly going to have to do some thinking about it now. Some pretty fast thinking, too.

Betsy saved the day, however, without even realizing it. Once she saw that we had reached our destination, she forgot all about Carla and her celebration.

''Okay, everybody, are we all clear on what we're supposed to do?'' she asked, her manner crisp and efficient. ''Sam, have you got your Polaroid camera?''

''Check,'' I replied, patting the tote bag I had looped over my shoulder.

''Carla, have you memorized the floor plan of Langtree Industries?''

''Check,'' she said. ''I know where everything is. The storage closets, the central files . . . even the rest rooms.''

Betsy and I both laughed.

''I guess we're all set, then. Let's go!''

Walking tall and looking very sure of ourselves, the

Bubble Gum Gang descended upon Langtree Industries. My heart was pounding, but I tried really hard not to let the way I was feeling show. I even managed to do a pretty good job.

"Hello, Ms. Mason," I greeted the receptionist who had worked at my father's company for something like ten years. She looked pleased to see me. She was a friendly woman, the type who was always marveling over how much I had grown and telling me what a fine young woman I was growing into.

"How nice to see you, Samantha," she said, sounding genuinely happy to see me.

I introduced Carla and Betsy, then said, "Is my dad in his office? He's expecting us."

"Oh, we're all expecting you," she returned. "In fact, your father sent out a memo two days ago, telling everyone in the company about your school project. Go right in."

To say that the employees of Langtree Industries were waiting for us would have been an understatement. I haven't felt so welcome since I was nine years old. Then, after spending two solid months at a French summer camp, I returned home to find that my family had planned a surprise "welcome home" party for me. As I filed through the building toward the back where my father's office is, just about everybody looked up and greeted us.

"Welcome to Langtree Industries," they all said, smiling.

Betsy grabbed me by the arm. "Sam," she whispered, "are you sure about this? How are we going to snoop around when everybody in this place is acting like we're royalty?''

"Betsy is right," Carla added, her voice also low. "What if we don't get a moment to ourselves?"

"Don't worry," I insisted. But my heart was sinking. She had a point. It *was* going to be hard to take a good look around. "Just be creative."

And that, I knew, was exactly what we were going to have to do. The only problem was that at the moment I didn't have a single idea in my head.

"There you are, Samantha!" my father boomed. He came around from behind his big desk and walked toward us. "Welcome to—"

"We know," I said, laughing.

"Hello, Mr. Langtree," Carla and Betsy said.

"Daddy, thanks again for letting us come to your office."

He waved his hand in the air. "It's my pleasure. Now I want you three to make yourselves at home. I've told all my employees about your visit, and every one of them is eager to help you find out anything you need to know."

"*Almost* every one of them," Betsy muttered. I would have jabbed her in the side, but she was standing too far away.

"We'd like to keep this informal," I told my father. "You know, just go off on our own, look around, watch people work. . . ."

"Be my guest," Daddy said. "Just holler if you need me."

"Oh, I'm sure we'll manage just fine on our own, Mr. Langtree," Betsy said with a big smile. "We'll tiptoe around so quietly that most people won't even realize we're here.''

I shooed my two pals out the door.

"Okay," I told them once we were out of earshot. "Let's break up and go off on our own, just as we planned.''

Betsy nodded. ''Right. I'm off to Accounting to see if I can see anything funny about the way the money is handled in the company.''

"And I'm heading off to Personnel,'' Carla said. "I'll try to ask some insightful questions. Maybe I'll be able to find out something that way.''

"Good,'' I said. "And I'll be a free agent, lurking in corners and slipping around the corridors. Who knows what I'll uncover?''

For the next hour, I did my best to find out what was going on behind the scenes at Langtree Industries. I did learn some interesting things—mostly about how the computer industry works. Unfortunately, none of what I was learning had anything to do with what I was trying to uncover.

I kept hoping that Carla and Betsy were having better luck. But at four-thirty, when we checked in with one another at the water fountain the way we had planned, their crestfallen faces told me that they weren't having any better luck than I was.

"So?" Betsy asked, looking at me hopefully. "Have you seen or heard anything suspicious?"

I shook my head. "I'm afraid not. How about you? Carla, did you learn anything interesting?"

She perked up. "I found out that nobody wants to be in charge of the company Christmas party because last year's was such a disappointment. I found out that the Xerox machine has been broken for two days, and everyone is going crazy. I also found out that a man named Charles Post is leaving the company. . . ."

"Really?" I asked excitedly. "Why?"

"He's going back to college to finish his degree."

I sighed. "How about you, Betsy? Did you find out anything?"

"Only that your dad's company is having some financial problems. But I guess you already knew that."

"So far, nothing," I said, more to myself than to my friends. "Well, we're just going to have to go back out there and keep trying."

"We'd better move fast," said Betsy, glancing at her watch. "The office closes in half an hour."

Part of me felt like giving up. But part of me felt like using that last half hour to the fullest. I wandered around the maze of offices, wondering how I could best do that. And then, all of a sudden, the mention of a familiar name stopped me in my tracks.

". . . the funny way Mr. McArdle is always acting," one of the secretaries was saying, her voice a near whisper.

I immediately looked over in her direction. She was talking to another secretary, who was holding a large stack of file folders.

"I want to hear more," said the second woman. "But I simply have to put these away in the storage closet."

My heart had started pounding. Suddenly, I knew that no matter what, I had to find out what these two employees were saying about Steve McArdle. Without a moment's hesitation, I headed toward the nearest storage closet. After checking around to make sure no one was watching, I ducked inside.

Fortunately, it was fairly large. It was almost a small storage room, one of those walk-in closets that two or three people could fit into at a time. Even though I was in a state of near panic, I was thinking very clearly. The first thing I did was reach up and unscrew the single light bulb in the ceiling. I tucked it away in the back of the closet. The second thing I did was crouch down inside, hiding behind a huge box of computer paper.

By now, my heart was pounding really loudly—so loudly, in fact, that I felt as if everybody in the entire building could hear it. I looked around, trying to calm myself by focusing on the shelves. It was hard to make anything out, since the only light coming in was a small crack underneath the door. I did catch sight of a dozen staplers, a carton of a hundred pencils, and the biggest box of paper clips I have ever seen in my life.

"Great," I muttered. "I feel like Mr. Homer, surrounded by paper clips."

But I quickly grew silent when the closet door opened. I leaned back even further, not wanting to be seen. I also stopped breathing.

"Oh, no!" cried the second secretary, the one carrying the folders. "The light in here is out again."

"I'll call maintenance," her friend offered. "Anyway, haven't you noticed anything strange about Mr. McArdle?"

"What do you mean?" She was sliding the file

folders onto a shelf about ten inches away from my head. Fortunately, between being absorbed in her conversation and not being able to see very well because of the lack of light, she didn't notice the blond head tucked underneath the carton of computer disks.

"Well . . ." The other secretary lowered her voice even more. "It's just that he's always so . . . so *secretive*. A lot of the time, he won't even let me answer his phone."

"Oh, he's probably just overly anxious. The type who's always trying to make a good impression on Mr. Langtree." She patted the file folders, then brushed her hands together. Just before she closed the door to the storage closet, I heard her say, "So what are you doing this weekend?"

Steve McArdle, acting strange. Acting secretive. I had heard it from a very good source, a woman who worked with him day in and day out . . . a woman whom he had told not to answer his telephone.

To say that I wanted to know more was, as they say, a real understatement. Suddenly I had this driving need to find out everything I could about Steve McArdle. After all, it wasn't only the secretary who had noticed his odd behavior. I thought about all the presents he was buying for his children. I had wondered then where all the extra money was coming from, and here I was, wondering the same thing all over again.

I peeked out of the storage closet, sneaking out when I saw no one was watching. Since it was the end of the day—a Friday, no less—everyone was busy finishing up last-minute details and getting ready to go home, not studying the closets to see if anyone had been lurking inside. Once I was in the clear, I plastered a big smile on my face and headed toward Steve McArdle's office.

I had told Betsy and Carla that we needed to be creative. Now, it was time for me to follow my own advice.

"Hi, Mr. McArdle!" I said boldly, striding right into his office.

"Samantha! What a nice surprise!" He had just hung up the phone, I noticed. Casually he tore a piece of paper off the pad of paper on his desk, folded it twice, and tucked it into his shirt pocket. "How is your little research project going?"

"Oh, fine. I'm sure that my friends and I are going to get an *A* after we write up our report. We're learning so much."

"Good, good. Well, if there's anything I can help you girls with . . ."

"Thank you, but the reason I'm here is to tell you that my father wants to see you."

"Your father? Certainly." He was already standing up, straightening his tie. Wearing a friendly smile, he added, "Whatever the boss wants!"

"See you later," I called after him as I watched him stride down the hall toward my father's office. What Dad was going to say when Steve McArdle unexpectedly showed up, I couldn't say. And at the moment, I didn't really care.

I had gotten what I wanted: a few minutes to look around Steve McArdle's office. The problem was, I didn't know where to begin. There was a tall file cabinet in one corner, but it would have taken me hours or even days to go through it. There was his desk, too, but I couldn't imagine sneaking around in there.

It was while I was wondering how exactly to start that the pad of paper on his desk caught my eye. I went over to it to take a closer look. True, he had torn off the top sheet, the one he had written on. But I had seen enough spy movies to know that the force of his pen would have left an imprint on the second page of the pad as well.

Sure enough, when I looked at it closely, I could see what he had written, only minutes before.

He had written, "C.M. Five-fifteen."

C.M. The same initials as Computer Masters. It could have simply been a coincidence, the initials of his dentist or his accountant or the place where he got his hair cut . . . but I wasn't willing to accept that without first doing a bit more investigating.

As I left his office, I was almost certain I had stumbled upon something important. I could hardly wait to tell Carla and Betsy. All of a sudden, I had a suspect.

"Follow that car!" I cried to the taxi driver, feeling like the star of an adventure movie.

The three of us were crammed into the backseat of a taxi, our faces pressed eagerly against the windows. It had been my idea to call for a taxi so we could slip out of my dad's office precisely when the time was right. And so far, so good. I watched as Steve McArdle left the building at five o'clock on the dot, went directly to his car, and headed toward the road that led to the next town—where Computer Masters, my father's main competitor, just happened to be located.

"I hope you're right about this hunch of yours," Betsy said. "What if it turns out Mr. McArdle is simply going to the dentist?"

Carla answered that one for me. "Then we won't have lost anything. But if it turns out that Sam's hunch *is* correct . . ."

Even though it wasn't particularly cold, I shivered. The idea of Steve McArdle turning out to be the person who was selling secrets from my father's company was nothing short of horrifying. Part of me hoped that I would turn out to be right, that I would have found out who the bad apple in the barrel was. But another part of me hoped that I would find I had been wrong about this man, the father of Jimmy and Patty and sweet little Willy.

"So far, he's heading straight in the direction of Computer Masters," Betsy observed. "Still, there are a lot of office buildings around there. It's too early to tell anything yet."

"It's not going to be too early for long," countered Carla. "Look! His car just turned into the parking lot of Computer Masters!"

My heart sank. Sure enough, Steve McArdle's car was pulling into an empty space right near the front door. But there was no time for sitting around, feeling bad. As the taxi let us out half a block away from where Mr. McArdle's car was parked, I leaned forward and snapped a few pictures of him going into the building with my Polaroid camera. Carla, meanwhile, paid the driver.

"Good luck, Sherlock Holmes!" he called over his shoulder with a grin. Then he sped away.

"Now what?" Carla asked. "Just because he's going into the building doesn't mean he's selling company secrets to your dad's competitor."

"Carla is right," Betsy agreed. "We can't go around making accusations until we're really sure."

"I know," I said. "And that's why we have to go inside."

"Go inside!" Betsy and Carla repeated in unison.

"That's right. Don't worry, I'll go first. After all, it *is* my father's company that's on the line. Besides," I added with a little laugh, "this whole thing was my idea in the first place, remember? Come on, follow me!" I only wished I felt as confident as I sounded.

Since it was five-fifteen on a Friday afternoon, it was no surprise to me that the office building was practically deserted. It was like school on a Friday: everybody dashed out right away, eager to get the weekend going. That was fine with me, since having nobody around made it that much easier for the three of us to do our sleuthing act.

I slipped inside first, my Polaroid camera in hand. Carla and Betsy were right behind. We all walked softly, staying close to the wall. I just hoped we wouldn't run into anybody. I didn't know about the others, but my mind was racing so fast that I didn't think I could come up with an excuse for what we were doing in there if my life—or my father's company—depended on it.

"That's him!" I suddenly cried, my voice a loud whisper. "I just heard Steve McArdle's voice!"

Sure enough, he was in someone's office, just around the corner from where we were standing. As I peeked through the doorway, I saw that the door to that office was almost closed. I couldn't see inside, but I could hear everything.

"Let's hide—quick," I commanded. Carla crouched down behind two file cabinets. Betsy slipped into a storage closet. I, meanwhile, ducked underneath a desk, just a few feet away from the office in which Steve McArdle was standing. On the wall right outside was a sign that read, "Todd Masters, President."

"Congratulations, Steve!" boomed the voice of a stranger. "Thanks to you, we're getting a real head start in the voice-activated computer business. Too bad we couldn't use the name, though. I really liked the ring of 'VAC-Man.' "

"Look, Todd," Mr. McArdle said impatiently. "Just give me my money. We had a deal, and I held up my end. Now it's time for you to come through with your end."

"Don't worry. I've got your money." The other man, Todd, chuckled coldly. "Money, money, money. It certainly makes the world go round, doesn't it, Steve? Here you go."

"Should I count it?"

"Oh, come on. You know you can trust me."

There was a long pause. I figured Steve McArdle was counting his money.

And then, "Perfect, Todd. Exactly the amount we agreed on."

"I told you you could trust me. But tell me. What are you going to do with all that money?"

"Actually, I plan to buy my three kids a swimming pool."

"A swimming pool!"

"That's right. A really fancy one. One of those concrete ones, built into the ground, with a deck all around."

The other man chuckled again. "Lucky kids. I just hope they appreciate what a loving father they have."

I felt like crying as I tucked my Polaroid back into my tote bag. I wouldn't be able to take any more pictures without being discovered, I realized. But that didn't matter. I had already gotten an earful—and two witnesses, to boot. There was no doubt in my mind that I had learned enough to be able to tell my father who the spy in his company was.

I only wished there were some way I could keep Jimmy, Patty, and Willy from finding out what kind of man their father really was.

I guess I should have been excited as I walked into my house a while later, the Polaroids I had taken in my hand and the entire conversation I had overheard in my head. Instead, my feet felt as if they were made of rock. The worst was yet to come, I knew. Finding out who the spy in my father's company was was one thing. Telling him was something else altogether.

I found my dad alone in the den, watching the news on television.

"Oh, hi, Samantha!" he greeted me. "How was your afternoon at my office? Helpful, I hope. But you girls certainly rushed out of there in a hurry. Couldn't wait for the weekend to start, huh?''

I sat down on a chair opposite him. ''That wasn't quite it, Daddy.'' Nervously I cleared my throat. ''You see, when I told you that Betsy and Carla and I wanted to come spend the afternoon at your company, it wasn't really because of any school project.''

''No?'' My father looked puzzled for a moment. Then he said, ''Oh, I see. You were just curious.''

''No, that's not quite it, either. You see, Daddy, I asked my friends to help me find out who the spy in your company was. You know, the person who's been selling secrets to your competitors—secrets like information about the new VAC-Man Langtree Industries has been developing.''

My father's expression had become one of astonishment. ''But, Samantha! That's not your problem! I don't want you to feel you have to—''

''Wait, Daddy.'' I held up my hands. ''Please, this is hard enough. Just let me tell you what we discovered, okay? And I might as well start with these.''

I handed over the Polaroid pictures I had taken, three of them showing Steve McArdle looking around nervously, then going inside the offices of Computer Masters.

''But these . . . what . . .'' my father sputtered.

I took a deep breath. And then I told him everything.

He didn't speak until I had finished. I half expected him to start yelling, or to race to the telephone to put in a furious call to Steve McArdle. Instead, he simply shook his head slowly. His voice was filled with sadness as he said, "But I *trusted* Steve McArdle. I always thought of him as one of my most loyal employees. Why, he's been with the company practically since I started it!"

"I know, Daddy," I said softly.

"My goodness, isn't there any such thing as loyalty anymore? Or is even that up for sale? Are Steve's values really so mixed up that he thinks it's more important to buy his kids a swimming pool than to show them that honesty is what matters? Honesty, and loyalty, and . . . and . . ."

"And spending time with the people you really care about," I finished for him. "Instead of wasting it finding ways to make more money, I wish Mr. McArdle would spend some time with his kids. They're the ones who need him. They're the ones who care about him. It's his family that matters, not selling out the company where he works just so he can buy them more toys and things they don't really need—or want."

"Well, honey, you've done a good job here," my father said, standing up. "I'll have to think about how to handle this. I suppose the first thing I need to do is talk to my lawyers."

He wandered out of the room, looking lost. I felt so bad for him. My poor father! Here he had been thinking that Steve McArdle was someone who was his true friend, someone whom he could count on, someone who believed in the same things he believed in. And now, he found out he had been betrayed. My heart went out to him.

Just then, the telephone rang. I picked it up. I didn't

really feel like talking to anybody, but I figured it would probably be Betsy or Carla, calling to find out how my father had taken the bad news.

Instead, in response to my sullen "Hello," I heard Kicky's chirpy voice.

"Oh, hi, Samantha! I just wanted to remind you that we're all meeting at my house at seven tonight." She giggled. "There's something I forgot to mention, too. Whenever we go to the movies, we just *have* to have popcorn. So make sure you bring along enough money to buy some for each of us. For yourself, too, of course," she added quickly.

As she was talking, something inside me was churning. Slowly, at first, as if something fuzzy was trying desperately to come into focus.

And then, there it was, as clear as the Polaroids I had taken. I realized that I had been doing the same thing as Steve McArdle! I had been sidestepping the people who really cared about me, my true friends. Instead I had been putting my energy into things that didn't matter . . . and trying to use money to buy friendship. Betsy and Carla had been right all along. It wasn't *me* that Kicky and Wendy and that whole crowd liked. It was my *money* . . . and what I could buy for them.

And I had let myself be taken in. I had so desperately wanted to believe that I mattered to them that I had been blinded to the things that really counted. Things like real, sincere, honest friendship. Just as Steve McArdle hadn't been able to see that it was his family that was most important, I hadn't been able to see the value of my true friends. And I had been hurting them in the same way that Steve McArdle had been hurting Jimmy, Patty, and Willy.

"Samantha, are you there?" Kicky asked, sounding annoyed. "You did hear what I just said, didn't you?"

I took a deep breath. And when I exhaled, I felt as if I had just woken up from a long, deep sleep.

"I won't be going to the movies with you and your friends tonight, Kicky. I have something much more important to do."

chapter
ten

"Sorry I'm late," I said breathlessly as I came dashing into Yo-Yo's Yogurt at ten minutes after seven.

Carla and Betsy were already there, sitting at the choice table, the one right next to the window. They were all dressed up, wearing their favorite sweaters and, of course, hair ornaments, courtesy of Ellsworth von Thornbottom. I was dressed up, too, in my favorite outfit. It was from an outrageous boutique in London—not at all the kind of thing girls around here were wearing.

"That's okay," Carla replied, beaming. "I'm just glad you're here."

"Yes," Betsy agreed. "We're glad you decided that this was where you wanted to be tonight, Samantha."

Slowly the meaning of their words dawned on me. "Wait a minute. Are you two saying . . . ?"

They both started to laugh. "That's right, Sam," said Carla. "We knew all about Kicky's invitation. If you can call it that."

"Right," Betsy agreed. "After all, since you were supposed to be the one to pay for everything . . ."

"But . . . but . . . how did you know?" I plopped into the empty chair, my mouth open in amazement.

"Are you kidding?" Carla said. "Good old Kicky has been bragging about it all week. Even to us."

"*Especially* to us," Betsy added meaningfully.

I buried my face in my hands. "Oh, boy," I breathed. "I am so embarrassed. You two must think I'm the jerk of the century. I'm surprised you'd even want to be in the same room as me after what I did."

Gently Betsy pulled my hands away from my face. "We're just glad you finally realized who your real friends are, Samantha."

"Boy, I'll say! I'm just sorry it took me so long to see what Kicky and her crowd are really all about." Shyly, I added, "And of course I've known all along what you two are all about. I'm just sorry I had to put you through this. I hope I didn't hurt you too much. If it makes you feel better, I think I'm the one who's suffered the most from not recognizing right off what was important to me."

"From what I know of life," Carla said earnestly, "there will always be Kickys and Wendys in the world."

I laughed. "Well, that's okay. At least, as long as there are *also* Carlas and Betsys in the world!"

"Speaking of loyalty," Betsy said, her tone suddenly serious, "how did your father react to the news about Steve McArdle?"

"He was really upset," I replied. "He had thought that Steve was somebody he could trust. I think he feels as if somebody kicked him in the stomach. I felt so bad that I was the one to tell him the bad news."

"I can imagine," Betsy said gently. "But it's still better that he know the truth."

"I'll say," Carla agreed. "Especially if he wants to hang on to his company."

I nodded, certain they were right. "I know. He was on the phone with his lawyers when I left tonight. What Steve McArdle was doing is very serious. There's going to be an investigation by the United States Attorney General's office. Selling corporate secrets is a very serious crime, you know. My dad says he'll probably end up going to jail, maybe for as long as three years. He'll have to pay a fine, too, somewhere in the hundreds of thousands of dollars."

"Wow!" Carla breathed. "That *is* serious."

"Well, tonight we're here to celebrate Carla," Betsy reminded us. "And, of course, her terrific achievement of losing five pounds."

"Here, here," I said. "Bring on the frozen yogurt!"

"It's funny," Carla observed, "but it turns out that healthy frozen yogurt with strawberries is just as tasty as fattening chocolate ice cream with hot fudge sauce . . . especially if you're eating it with two great people!"

"I'll say," I agreed heartily. "Nothing feels as good as true friendship. And nobody knows that as well as I do!"

That, as they say, is a real understatement.

About the Author

Cynthia Blair grew up on Long Island, earned her B.A. from Bryn Mawr College in Pennsylvania, and went on to get an M.S. in marketing from M.I.T. She worked as a marketing manager for food companies but has abandoned the corporate life in order to write. She lives on Long Island.

Follow the exciting adventures
of the irrepressible Pratt Twins

THE BANANA SPLIT AFFAIR

What happens when identical twins with completely different personalities switch places? In their very first adventure, the Pratt twins are each convinced the other has a better life. Susan is a straight-A student and a talented artist, but she's painfully shy. Christine is outgoing, fashionable, and popular with the boys. Chris bets her twin they can pull off a switch, and there is much more at stake than just a banana split.

THE HOT FUDGE SUNDAY AFFAIR

Christine Pratt can't believe it when she's chosen to be the honorary queen of her town's Centennial Week. She realizes she would never have been chosen without her identical twin sister's help, and she has a plan. During Centennial Week they take turns being Christine, but the girls learn the hard way that you can't fool everyone all of the time.

STRAWBERRY SUMMER

The Pratt twins land jobs as counselors at Camp Pinewood and envision a summer filled with sun and fun and strawberries. When they learn someone has been sabotaging the camp, Susan and Christine decide to investigate, with doubly hilarious results!

THE PUMPKIN PRINCIPLE

Chris is determined to make this Halloween dance extra special—after all, it's her senior year and B. J. Wilkins, a new guy at school, has noticed her. But what does it mean when she sees B. J. deep in conversation with Susan? Whatever he's up to— and no matter how cute he is—the Pratt twins are not going to let him get away with this. So they plan a little surprise for B. J., but they get their own surprise at the Halloween dance.

THE MARSHMALLOW MASQUERADE

It's Homecoming time and that means dances and dates and boys. Susan decides that Chris, as the braver of the two twins, should dress as a boy and infiltrate the enemy camp. So Chris becomes "Charlie" Pratt, a cousin who'll be going to school while Chris is out with the flu. But little do the twins realize that being a boy is trickier than they thought.

THE CANDY CANE CAPER

Susan and Christine spend Christmas in beautiful, snowy Vermont with their grandparents. The twins discover that someone is embezzling funds from a children's hospital that will close if something isn't done fast. The girls get the whole town of Ridgewood involved in a bazaar to raise money for the hospital. They put their "double" identities to good use when they decide to do some sleuthing of their own to save the day!

THE DOUBLE DIP DISGUISE

Christine and Susan Pratt spend the summer before college with their grandparents on picture-perfect Seagull Island off the coast of North Carolina. Chris goes to work in the town's only ice-cream parlor, while Susan takes care of the Hollingworth children. The Hollingworths live in a spooky Victorian house, and Chris and the children are forbidden to enter a wing of the house. When the family throws a big benefit ball, Susan decides a sister substitution is in order to solve this mystery.

THE POPCORN PROJECT

The twins visit Los Angeles to help their sick aunt, and one of the first people they meet is Donald Franklin, a movie executive who asks for their help. His daughter Jennifer has been working as a guide at his studio and she's not been herself lately. The girls go behind the scenes to stop a dangerous and desperate man with a deadly secret.

THE APPLE PIE ADVENTURE

The Pratt twins move to New York City, where Chris begins college, and Susan enrolls in the Morgan School of Art. At an exhibit for Susan's school, the twins meet formidable Barbara Mason convinced she's dealing in stolen antiquities, they begin to investigate. The trail leads them aboard a luxury liner bound for South America, and Susan must do some quick thinking to save Chris from being shipped to Peru.

THE JELLY BEAN SCHEME

The twins are thrilled to learn that a town history they wrote is being considered for a National History prize, and they get to fly down to New Orleans for the contest. When a fellow historian who is researching the exotic and mysterious world of voodoo disappears, the twins suspect the worst. Ignoring dire warnings to keep far away from the unknown dangers of New Orleans, Christine and Susan begin a perilous search for their missing friend.

THE LOLLIPOP PLOT

Chris and Susan love going to college in the Big Apple, but they are excited about Homecoming Weekend at their old high school. The dynamic duo returns home, only to discover a plan afoot to harm the mayor. The twins cannot resist some amateur sleuthing, but they didn't know about the haunted house or the very real danger awaiting them.

THE COCONUT CONNECTION

The twin's parents surprise them with a Hawaiian vacation for Christmas—surely no harm can come to them on these exotic islands. Then Chris meets the nephew of a coconut tycoon and discovers trouble in paradise. The twins are determined to unravel this mystery, even if it means trespassing on sacred land and unleashing an ancient curse.

CYNTHIA BLAIR

Call 1-800-733-3000 to order by phone and use your major credit card. Please mention interest code KAF-1192Z to expedite your order. Or use this coupon to order by mail.

____ GOING SOLO	70360-6	$3.95
____ A SUMMER IN PARIS	70393-2	$3.99

Bubble Gum Gang

____ THERE'S NO SUCH THING AS A HAUNTED HOUSE	70399-1	$3.99
____ CHOCOLATE IS MY MIDDLE NAME	70400-9	$3.99

The Pratt Twins

____ THE BANANA SPLIT AFFAIR	70175-1	$3.50
____ HOT FUDGE SUNDAY AFFAIR	70158-1	$3.99
____ STRAWBERRY SUMMER	70183-2	$2.95
____ THE PUMPKIN PRINCIPLE	70205-7	$2.95
____ MARSHMALLOW MASQUERADE	70217-0	$3.99
____ THE CANDY CANE CAPER	70221-9	$2.95
____ THE PINK LEMONADE CHARADE	70258-8	$3.50
____ THE DOUBLE DIP DISGUISE	70256-1	$3.50
____ THE POPCORN PROJECT	70309-6	$3.99
____ APPLE PIE ADVENTURE	70308-8	$3.99
____ THE JELLY BEAN SCHEME	70351-7	$3.95
____ THE LOLLIPOP PLOT	70377-0	$3.95
____ THE COCONUT CONNECTION	70378-9	$3.99

Name _____

Address _____

City _____ State _____ Zip _____

Please send me the FAWCETT BOOKS I have checked above.

I am enclosing	$ _____
plus	
Postage & handling*	$ _____
Sales tax (where applicable)	$ _____
Total amount enclosed	$ _____

*Add $2 for the first book and 50¢ for each additional book.

Send check or money order (no cash or CODs) to:
Fawcett Mail Sales, 400 Hahn Road, Westminster, MD 21157

Prices and numbers subject to change without notice.
Valid in the U.S. only.
All orders subject to availability.